From the Heart

By

Yolanda P. Tyson

To order additional copies of this book, contact:
1177 6th Ave 5th Floor
New York, NY 10036, USA
Phone: (+1 347-922-3779)
info@proislepublishing.com

PROISLE PUBLISHING

Content

1. Police Search
2. My Son
3. Uninvited Guest
4. Mother Knows Best
5. Daddy's Home
6. Can't Be Ignored
7. What Is A Friend?
8. My Mother's Daughter
9. Can't Take No More
10. SOS
11. Deadbeat Dads
12. My Own Woman
13. My Dad
14. ABC's Of Success
16. Obsessed
17. Tough Love
18. Acrophobia
19. Facing Fears
20. Obesity Depression
21. Too Much Sugar
22. I'm So Beautiful
23. I Love You
24. I Feel Good
25. Proud Mom
26. Slugs
27. Grandparents
28. Forgiven Betrayal
29. Work Out
30. Leave Me Be
31. Too Much Isn't Right
32. Don't Tell Me No!!
33. Time
34. Comfort Zone
35. In The Dark
36. Sex Addict
37. "Always And Forever"
38. My First Love
39. Forever Young
40. Love Or Hate?
41. Don't Criticize
42. Good Fruit?
43. Shut Up
44. New Year's Day
45. Secret Lovers
46. A Segregated Family
47. What Next?
48. R.I.P.
49. Mistletoe
50. Bumble Bees
51. Secret Crush
52. Baby Number Four?
53. Move Over
54. Daddy's Girls
55. Too Good To Be True
56. It's Not That Serious
57. Please Don't Go
58. The Right Choice
59. I'm Not My Mother
60. Always Falling
61. Family
62. I Want Peace
63. Good People
64. Sheba
65. Oreo
66. Accept Your Own Advice "Never Say Can't"...
67. Apple Tree
68. It Ain't Easy

69. Go Away
70. A Good Man
71. To The Top
72. Justice
73. Philadelphia
74. Queen Mom
75. Christmas Day
76. I Want To Be Loved
77. I'm Going Home
78. Love Or Lust
79. Get Out
80. A Closed Mouth
81. Happy Birthday
82. Running Water
83. Nights Of Passion
84. A Mother's Nightmare
85. My Way
86. What Would You Do?
87. Again I Tried
88. Zodiac Signs
89. A Friend In Jesus
90. Halloween
91. Momma's Boy
92. Scared
93. Lose Weight Gain
94. Anything For You
95. The First Day
96. My First Baby
97. Far And Near
98. Let Them Be Kids
99. Invisible Mother
100. Out Of Control
101. A New Baby
102. What If?
103. The Perfect Day
104. Kissing You
105. Skin Deep
106. Sexual Feelings
107. Privacy Please
108. On My Mind
109. The Brothers
110. Reunited
111. Thanksgiving Day
112. Stolen Life
113. So Cruel
114. Is He Really Here?
115. Insecurity
116. Peer Pressure
117. Could It Be?
118. In My Life Again
119. I Want You Back
120. Beautiful Eyes
121. It's Not Right
122. No Heat
123. Mother's Day
124. Fuel To The Fire
125. My Sweet Valentine
126. Let It Snow
127. I'm Sorry
128. Am I Good?
129. My Little Kittens
130. One More Chance
131. If You Were Mine
132. Why Now?
133. Tears Of Love
134. Every time I See You
135. Take Me Home
136. In Love Alone
137. Can't Hide Love
138. The Way I Feel
139. Busted
140. Should We Be Together?
141. It's You
142. Trapped
143. The Way I Feel

144. Should We Be Together?
145. We Are Family
146. Night Of Passion
147. I Want You
148. Silent Tears
149. Undercover Lovers
150. Moonlit Skies
151. Lonely Memories
152. Butterfly
153. Wanting More
154. Working Out
155. Forever Mine
156. My Hero
157. Socks
158. Feeling The Wind
159. M.Y.O.B.
160. Identity Theft
161. All Alone
162. Goodbye
163. Top Of The Class
164. Too Much
165. Irresponsible
166. Fate Or Love
167. Beggars
168. Why Want More?
169. A Sunny Day
170. I'm Free
171. Unexpected Pregnancy
172. I Need A Job!
173. Marriage
174. "Crazy People"
175. Enzo And Chyna
176. Holding Me Back
177. It's Fine
178. P.I.T.A
179. Deadbeat Moms
180. In The Mirror

181. The Love I Lost
182. Seizures
183. Have You Ever?
184. What's Wrong?
185. Perfect Strangers
186. Love Letter
187. You Must Obey
188. Moving On
189. I Got It Bad
190. Irreplaceable
191. God's Miracle
192. Thieving Angels
193. Favoritism
194. I'm Me
195. Depression Hurts
196. The Reverend's Daughter
197. We're Gonna Make It
198. Rejected
199. Until It's Gone
200. Back & Forth
201. Phat Bitches
202. Tell Me Why
203. Getting Played
204. You Don't Know Me
205. A Hero
206. I Wish
207. Emotional Roller Coaster
208. Make It Last
209. Rainy Days
210. I'm Missing You
211. I'm Ready
212. Hard Times
213. Being Fooled
214. My Sick Baby
215. Go Away
216. Lock It Down

217. The Man Whom
     Cried
218. I'm Coming
219. A New Year
220. Ain't Getting It Right?
221. WWJD?
222. My Husband
223. Chauvinism
224. Grateful
225. Slow Down
226. Quit Now
227. Always Be First
228. Follow Your Heart
229. Unhappy
230. Too Much
231. Just Me
232. "Mommy And Me
     Day"
233. Got Screwed?
234. Family Secrets
235. Unappreciated
236. Feed Me Now
237. Love Me Or Leave Me
238. Can't Take No More

I'm a Poet

I'm a poet, I know it,
I'm not afraid to show it.

Most of the time, I write what's on my mind,
About the feelings I hide inside of me into poetry.

Others are made up and from other stories
With a little twist, I also wrote about my first kiss.

What inspired me to write poetry was when I was
A teen, I always wrote in my diary.

As I was getting older, I performed on stage @
Poetry bars, that was so much fun.

My poetry is written from the heart, I knew
I was a poet after the first one.

Police Search

North, South, East, West, the sirens
So loud nobody can rest. Their flashing
Light brighten the night.

Helicopters flying loudly across
The great blue sky. All of this noise
And nobody why
Children so confused, they start to cry.

Most people stay inside of the house,
While others stand outside to
See what the fuss is all about.

My Son

Jewel – precious thing
Elations – High spirits
Resplendent – Brilliant
Eager – full of desire
Macabre – imagination
Intelligent – quick @ understanding
Adorable – Love intensely
Handsome – Fine Appearance

This is my Son, My Only One.
I Love to watch him grow and play.
He learns something new every day.
He's special and unique in his own way.

It felt good to feel his movement in my belly,
I see him move too, I was so excited,
I didn't know what to do
When he was placed in my Arms, my Smile
Was wide as the sea, because God

Brought him here just for me.
He's my bundle of Joy, and a pita,
But he's still my baby boy.

Uninvited Guest

Don't you just hate uninvited Guest?
They always leave your home a mess.
They never show up alone, they come with
Family and friends, then the trouble begins
Because they roam in your home.

Uninvited guests can't pay rent, a bill, nor are they
Able to put food on the table but yet;
They relax and chill. Sometimes they even eat up your food;
Now you know that's rude. Time to get a cat, imagine that

It feels good that I caught them all because
They're very fast and small. I can finally lay down and
Rest because I have no more uninvited guest.

Mother Knows Best

Never tell a mother about her children,
Because you'll never win. She's there from the
Beginning to the end. She knows what to do
And how to take care of them.

She has the unconditional love within her heart,
A mother knows best right from the start.
A mother's work is never done, even when they're
Grown and living on their own.

Daddy's Home

Daddy's home to stay for good. He may not be
Biological, but he does the things
A father should. He decided to be there because
The father doesn't care and can't be found anywhere

My children get so happy and excited to hear his name
And to see his face; you can feel the love all over the place.
He may not be a father, but we know he'll be a
Terrific dad. We love him and he's my
Best friend I ever had.

Can't Be Ignored

You talk about me, call me out of my name,
When things go wrong, you make me the blame,
You talk to me and treat me any kind of way,
And expect me to have nothing to say.

I'm not gonna allow myself to be taken advantage of,
I don't need you to love me, I have my own family,
"What goes around, comes around," so everything
You do is gonna come right back to you

I don't care that you're old, the way you
Treat me is really cold. You need to know your place
And stay out of my face.

What Is A Friend?

A friend is someone whom be there.
When times are good and bad, including
When you're happy or sad.

A friend is someone whom keeps it real.
Never tell a lie, but always tell the truth,
No matter what's the outcome and won't
Judge whom you are and where you come from.

A friend don't criticize how you look, dress, nor
Whether your home is in a mess.
A friend doesn't start trouble but in need
They'd be there on the double

A friend is open, honest, loyal, true and stay by your
Side no matter what you'd go through.
I have a friend, we're very close.
Our kids are friends and that's what
We love most.

My Mother's Daughter

My mother's daughter is a kind, sweet girl,
But not a lot of people is welcome into her world.

She has been taken for granted many times before,
Calling her names while pushing her through the door

People threw her issues in her face when it wasn't
Their place. They even tried putting her down.
Stomping on her head when she fell on the ground.

There are times when she is rude with an
Attitude and other times when she just broke down
And cried, because of all these feelings she holds inside,
But she doesn't worry
Because GOD is on her side.

Can't Take No More

Someone; Please help me; I'm about
To give up. My life is getting too tough and
I don't want it to get rough.

I'm so stressed because my life is in such
A big mess. I was supposed to be happy,
What Happened to that?

I'm so miserable my mind wanders
Off track. I can't take no more; I feel so
Frustrated, I want to break down the door.

When I become successful, those whom
Refuse to help me will be eliminated.

SOS

When I was a teen, things weren't going my way,
People were always mean, I cried every day.

I was always played for a fool.
My heart always gotten broken before
One word was even spoken

I even gotten embarrassed while I was in school
And that wasn't cool. Now as an adult, nothing
Has changed, everything is still the same,
Except I don't give anyone my heart, because I don't
Want it ripped apart.
This doesn't make any sense that I'm dealing
With the S.O.S. Only this time, I'm aware if
He doesn't care because my love, I don't share.

Deadbeat Dads

Why even bother, if you weren't ready to be a father?
Your kids and their mothers need you,
You should be ashamed of all the stress
You put them through.

You say "you care" but nobody can find you anywhere.
Why keep making babies, when your
Mind is filled with maybes.

My Own Woman

Why can't I make my own decisions about me?
I want to live my life the way I want it to be.
People telling me what to do, where to go, how to be,
How to act and how to dress, my life
Is just in a big mess. I am grown. I need to be alone,
On my own and away from you. I'm fed up with you
Telling me what to do.

I can't wait until the day I can move away.
I can come and go wherever and whenever I please.
I'm getting my own place because I'm my own
Woman and I want you out of my face.

# My Dad

My dad is one of the best friends I ever had;
I think about him often whenever we're apart,
He'll always have my heart.

When I'm feeling down, I get so excited just
To see him come around. I enjoy the time
We spend together, I'll always love my dad forever.

ABC's Of Success

Acknowledge their skills

Believe in their goals

Cheer for them when they do well

Do not put them down because of weakness

Educate them as much as you can

Forbid them to be friends with hoodlums

Guide them in the right path for achievement

Help them when they need it

Inform them they can do anything

Jubilate when they learn something new

Know not to put a strain on their brain

Lift their self-esteems

Monitor them while they're learning

"Never say can't"

Offer your help it they need it

Perceive their knowledge

Quote things that will make them feel good

Reassure them they can do it

Support their decisions no matter how they make it

Think of all the possibilities

Understand that there will be hard times

Venture and believe anything can be done

Walk with them as they follow their dreams

Xercise their minds as they grow

Yearn to be the best

Zero doubt about their accomplishments.

If parents and family follow these rules;

Children can succeed in any career they choose.

All children are very smart.

We should trust and believe in them from

The bottom of our hearts.

Don't just be a parent,

But a friend work with them and

Stand by their side until the very end.

Obsessed

Back off! You're crowding my space,
I don't need you in my face,
24/7 you always call then you wanna come by,
Without knowing a reason why.

I no longer want you to be with me,
And that isn't a maybe. I met you just a month ago,
You already wanna get married and have a baby,
You are crazy.

I'm not the only person in the world and certainly
Not the best. What is it about me that makes you
So obsessed? You may not recognize; but
You're making me stressed.

I don't want nor need it in my life and I certainly
Don't want nor do I need you. We didn't even go out so
I don't understand what this is obsession is all about.

Tough Love

All parents love their children,
But some of them are out of control,
Disobedient, and don't care.
What's it to do then?
Let them rule over your life and not listen to you?
How long are you gonna let them keep it up before you kick their
butt?

Kids say what they wanna say,
Do whatever they wanna do,
But still you love them more and more every day.
Don't beat them too much,
Because they'll take it as child abuse,
Then they'll be running loose and don't know what to do.

Acrophobia

I've been afraid of heights for a very long time,
I won't go up high even if I were paid,
Getting on a swing, don't mean a thing,
When it gets too high, it's time, for me to get low,
Get off the swing and go.

When I get picked up by someone, it's not much for
Standing on a chair feels weird. Climbing a ladder,
Isn't a laughing matter, supposed it isn't
Strong and it falls to the ground, then I'll just
Be lying around.

Facing Fears

For many years, I've been afraid to go way up high,
Almost like I could touch the sky.

One day I got on a Ferris wheel and all of the cars
Looked like toys, women and men looked
Like girls and boys.

Although, I did panic, it really wasn't that bad
It was one of the best experiences I ever had.

Obesity Depression

Depression really makes me feel weak,
Whenever I'm down, I always go get something to eat,
My depression has lasts for years, and I don't
Feel so needed now. Every now and then, I cry
So many tears.

I often diet and exercise, but I still feel the same inside
And haven't changed the way I look on the outside.

Every time I lose weight, I gain two times as much
Back. I feel so bad that I can't get rid of all of
This fat. For a while, I stayed away from snacks,
But then recently I went back.

Deep down inside, I always complain because I don't
Feel the same. Even before I fall asleep, I have
To get something to eat because this depression
Makes me weak.

Too Much Sugar

On a nice and hot day, people would like to have a nice
And cold drink. It may look good to the naked eye,
But it's really not as good as it should

Take a sip, then you'll see, it doesn't taste the way
It should be. So much for quenching thirst because
These drinks, taste the worse.

I'm So Beautiful

I'm so beautiful, can't nobody tell me nothing,
I admire myself looking @ my reflection in the mirror,
I look in the mirror 24/7

Styling my hair, wearing make-up, putting on jewelry
Doesn't make me, it's my beauty and the smile
On my face that can't be replaced.

I am beautiful, inside and out, can't nobody
Tell me what I'm about.

I'm so beautiful in my own way,
I get more beautiful, loving myself
More and more every day.

I Love You

I love you so much, more than anything in this world.
If you only knew the feelings I have for you.
When you touch me, my heart pounds.
I melt @ the way your voice sounds.

Sometimes I call you without having anything to say,
Just to hear you talk all day.
I love you and I want you to love me too,
Then you'll see we were meant to be.

I Feel Good

Today I went shopping for new clothes and
When I was done, I had to make another run

I went to the salon to get my hair done, that was fun,
Still I wasn't through, I've gotten a manicure,
Pedicure, and a facial wax too.

After I got out of the shower, I was the lady
Of the hour. I was feeling good the whole day
And everything was going my way.

Proud Mom

Every day I love to watch him grow,
The more I teach him, the more he know
He's in a higher stage, then other children his age

He amazes me to watch himself dress, but the
Way he eats is such a big mess,
He doesn't always do as he's told, but we
Keep each other warm when it's cold
And much more when he gets old.

I'm so proud to be his mom. He
Makes me smile all of the time.

Slugs

They are so slimy and disgusting,
I get paranoid just being around one,
Slugs isn't only slimy, some of them are very big
And the thought of being near them makes
Me itch and twitch.

I don't care what anyone says; slugs are creepy,
They really do creep me out, when I see one
I start to panic and shout.

So what they're just snails without their shells,
I don't like snails either. I can't see how people
Can eat them. They're nasty and slimy,
I definitely don't want them near me.

Grandparents

They are the best, they are always there in the time of need
And do all they can to help you succeed

Sometimes they are in a good mood and sometimes
They're not, but they'll give you all the love they got.

Grandparents have feelings too,
So watch what you say or do,
No matter what you go through

Forgiven Betrayal

For many years, you caused me to cry so many tears,
You mistreated me, day in and day out
But not one time did I scream and shout.

You stole from me. I gave you my heart
And you tore it apart. You aren't the person I
Thought you would be. I'm not gonna dwell
On the past, because I know my hurt
And pain won't last.

I forgive you, for all that you put me through,
But I'm fed up of taking care of you and
Dealing with the crazy things you do.

Work Out

Three times a week, I like to go to the gym.
I'd be there 3 or more hrs.
Feels so good gaining energy. Losing calories
And weight makes me feel great.

Sweating from head to toe, lets me know,
That the time spent @ the gym isn't a waste.
When I'm stressed, being @ the gym,
Is the right place. I like to sweat,
Because when I do, I feel real good
And it really raised my confidence.

Although sometimes it makes me feel
Better, I don't look better @ at all.
Looking at myself, doesn't look like I've
Lost a pound. I'm still the same size,
My clothes still fit, I'm starting too really
Feel like shit. And family isn't any help
They keep throwing it in my face
That I have a big waist.

When will they realize, that everyone
Isn't meant to be the same size.

Leave Me Be

Why do you always bother me? Am I the only
Person you see? Why are you always calling my
Phone, when I wanna be left alone?

Stop worrying about what I do. It's not your place,
So stay out of my face. My life has nothing
To do with you, and your life has nothing to do with me,
So leave me be.

I'm my own person, you can't change
Anything about me. I'm gonna stay the same
This is the way I really feel. This isn't a game.
It's so real, I'm fed up with your stalking
And lies, so keep on walking while
Saying your goodbyes.

Too Much Isn't Right

After the first one, I thought I was done,
But then I got two, I still wasn't through
So I had three, still it wasn't enough for me.

Then I drank four and still wanting more
After I had five, I took another dive. I had six,
That was just too much to mix.

When I had seven, I started sweating.
I had eight, than it was too late, I was tore, I
Didn't think I wanted anymore, but I had nine, I
Wasn't feeling so fine. When I had ten that was the end.
I was so sick, I didn't know where to begin.

Don't Tell Me No!!

Don't tell me No! For I am your mother
And you have no other. You are my child and
That's the way it go.

Do As I say Not As I do. I want to have
A better life for you.

I know I may seem to be mean, but I'm
Only doing the Right thing.

So as a Parent and your mother, I'm teaching you
The Right way instead of the wrong.

So, As long As you're my child
Don't tell me NO!

Time

The clock is ticking and time is running out.
I have so many sights to see and many places
To go where I haven't been yet

Most Places I want to go, I don't know how to get there
Because it's too far away from home.
This Big City, and I've been nowhere because
Getting there is too much carfare

I would like to travel, go places and do different
Things, but I don't know what the outcome brings. It
Just might be fun, maybe even better if
I go with someone.

Comfort Zone

This is my Comfort Zone...
Peace and quiet with nobody home.
I wanna sit back, relax, and pop some popcorn,
Get a soda, and watch a movie.

My Comfort Zone...
Is unplugging the phone, so I can be Alone.
Going to sleep without counting sheep.

The best comfort zone...
Is being Able to lay down, walking around,
In my night clothes and socks,
Locking the doors hoping nobody knocks.

My Comfort Zone...
Is being Left Alone.

In The Dark

When people see me, they assume I'm happy, because I
Have a family. Deep down inside, I have no pride. I have
Low self-esteem, I guess my life isn't as perfect
As it may seem.

While in public, I pretend my life is Alright, but I
Still cry @ night. Though I read my bible, I feel I have
NO REASONS left for me to live. I don't even love myself,
So how can I love someone else, when I have
No love to give?

Sex Addict

Every time you touch me, I don't want you to let me go.
The passion I feel when you're inside of me,
With you is where I want to be.

I want to feel your lips, from my neck
Down to my hips. Your tongue between my thighs,
Than into my clit, than I start to suck on your dick.

Now that my Pussy is nice n wet, I'm gonna
Make it a night you won't forget. A minute later
There's a knock on the door. A girl asks
"Is there room for one more?"

So now it's a threesome and this is so much fun
Kissing her, sucking her breast and licking the rest.
The mood is so right, I could go all night.

"Always And Forever"

This is such a beautiful song. I can listen to it all day long.
While planning A Romantic night, "Always and Forever",
Always sets the mood right.

Want something straight from the heart, but don't
Know where to start? Put on this CD and every word
Will be heard.

On My Wedding day, this is the song I want to play
"Always and forever" is the perfect song for couples
"Whom are in "in love." It expresses the way you know that
Those feelings are very real.

My First Love

I love her, She loves me, I promise
To be the best man I could be. I may be young,
But I know what I want in my life.
I want her to be my wife.

Our Moms are the best of friends.
If it wasn't for them, we would've never met.
That's a night I'll never forget.
I love to look into her pretty eyes.
Every time I see her, it's always a surprise.
She's not only my first girlfriend, she's also
My first love. She's my gift from GOD
In the heavens above.

Forever Young

No matter what my Age, the feeling of me being
Young will always stay the same.
I love working out. Feeling and looking good
Is what it's All About.

Most people says "I don't look my Age, I look
So young." When I look into the mirror,
I see a special glow in my face. Being
Forever young is in my place.
I always gain my confidence when people
Give me compliments.
I don't worry about scars and wrinkles
Because my looks don't change @ All.

Love Or Hate?

Once there was a married man. He Loved his wife, he
Also promised to be with her for life. He showered
Her with gifts and flowers. Now he stays out all kinds
Of hours. When he finally comes home, from leaving his
Wife alone, he has no explanation for this situation.
He didn't say one word. She thought it's about time
For her voice to be heard.

She asked, "Do you still Love me?" He said "Of course",
She then said "I want a divorce". He said
"Good night", and turned out the light.

Don't Criticize

Wow! This is sad, I never knew things would be
This bad. I used to think some People lied just to
Get over, but you'll never know until it hangs
Over your shoulder.

You'll never know how people felt unless you experience
The situation yourself. Not only I felt bad, but I also
Felt so sad. It was the worse feeling I ever had.

Good Fruit?

Don't you just love when you go pick out some
"Fresh fruit" from the "market?"

They looks so good and fresh, but when you get
It home it's in a mess.

You expect it to be so sweet and juicy, but instead
It's sour and dry.

How about others? When it's supposed to be
Solid on the outside and juicy on the inside,
It's the total opposite. It feels too wet
And mushy and isn't even sweet.
It's a waste of money and something good to eat.

Shut Up

People say the dumbest things, without knowing what
The outcome brings. A person can only take so much,
So a person should just shut up to avoid causing
Trouble. Some people even like to make smart remarks,
But try to stay positive and have a good heart,
Should just shut up and play your part.

Even though most of the time, you don't allow people to just
Say anything, keep cool, it'll work out one day you'll see. So just
Shut up so you won't say the wrong thing back without
Knowing how the other person will react. Shut up, they'll
Probably just take it the wrong way. So watch what you say
And stay cool, so you won't look like a fool.

New Year's Day

A New Year, A new me, I'm ready to become the
Person I was meant to be. It's time for a new heart
And this is how I'll start. I'll have joy instead of
Sorrow, and thanking GOD that I see tomorrow.

A chance to empty my bowl of sadness and fill it up
With happiness. Swallow my pride and express my
Feelings I hide inside.

A new year; not just for me, but also for my family.
We can find a way to get closer than ever,
To love each other more and be together forever

Secret Lovers

Two, "Married" couples for many, many, years:
Both of them have kids. One Couple have six while
The other have five, but the secret Lovers share
Four, each one wanting more.

When their secret is out and the true feelings start
To show. The faithful and loyal husband and wife,
Both said "you have to go and get out of my life."

So they took their kids and packed their things, moved
In together and lived happily ever after.

A Segregated Family

We used to be close,
Having a family reunion every year.

Where's the love that we used to share?
Nobody is willing to go anywhere.
Where's the Love we used to share?

We haven't had a family reunion in years,
The Last one we had, hardly nobody came,
And it was such a shame.

For   de,
Especially for so much wasted food.
We rarely keep in touch,
But always come together when it's a
Funeral, which isn't funny.

Most calls are being made is all about
Wanting money. When will the
Segregation end and we come together
As a family again?

What Next?

I've gotten my diploma, college degrees, scholarships, and
A few trades and still I can't get a job, but what about
My career? It seems like my accomplishments isn't
Going anywhere.

I have all of these bills, the mortgage, rent and car
Payments without a job. I can't make any arrangements
I hope I can get a job soon because these bills
Can't pay themselves and I won't depend on anyone else.

R.I.P.

As the years go by, I still wonder why; why was it
You whom had to go? Because I miss you so. There's
Nobody alive whom could ever love me the way you do
Because your love was unconditional and true. You were
There when I shed a tear, when I was scared you
Taught me not to fear.

When I had a bad dream, you showed me that it wasn't
As bad as it may seem, it feels like it was only yesterday
You went away. I still miss and think about you every day.
It's like our family is torn apart because you're not here,
But always in my heart.

Even though, the pain still hurts inside, knowing that
I don't have you by my side. You'll always be
Remembered and never forgotten, it will last forever
And ever because in a new life, again we'll be together.

This is a poem, I dedicate, to all of my loved ones that I have lost.

Mistletoe

Underneath the mistletoe, there are
A few things I'd like for you to know...

Underneath the mistletoe
Let's share our love and watch it grow.

Underneath the mistletoe, I'm yours
And you are mine. I like the way
You caress my spine.

Underneath the mistletoe, I want you to love
Me much more than you ever did before,
Love me all day and night so we'll
Make the mood right.

Underneath the mistletoe, I can't hide
The emotions I feel inside. I have
To let them out, so I can show you what my feelings are all about.

Bumble Bees

Thru the flowers around the trees
You can hear the sound of buzzing Bees.
Some of them make honey, but when they
Sting, it isn't funny.

When the weather gets cold, the move away
But always return on a nice spring day
Most people like honey. So rich and sweet. Put
Honey on anything, it becomes a tasty treat.

Secret Crush

I like you and I hope you like me too. We're Always
Around each other almost every day. Seeing you
Takes my breath Away. When you smile, I start to
Smile and it lights up my world @ the thought of
Being your girl. Your one and only lover and there'd
Be no other.

Whenever I'm cold my teeth chatter, but when
I'm with you, it doesn't matter. We shouldn't be
Together, but I'm willing to take that risk, starting
With a kiss.

Baby Number Four?

Oh my goodness, not again, I thought my life of bottles
And diapers have come to an end.

Being up all day and not being able to go to sleep @night,
Now that ain't right.

Today is my 1st ultrasound and what I saw will
Really turn my life around.

I thought I was getting baby number four, but
The GYN says "there's one more".

Move Over

Move Over! And let me take my place
I don't need you telling me what to do.
Move Over! Stop Boguarding my Authority.
For I am his mother and there is no other.
As you can plainly see, my child has only
One mother, and that's me.

Move Over! For all of your children are grown.
Well it's my turn now, so leave me Alone.
What you're doing isn't cool, you're making
Me feel like a fool.

Move Over, I know you love my child.
I love him 100,000 times as much
But right now I have that motherly touch
And I'm proud.

Move Over! I understand you wanna be here
For him and that's fine, but in GOD's eyes
And his choice, this child is mine.

Daddy's Girls

The Perfect trio,

Three beautiful girls living in a big state trying to make it through

this big world but we still communicate.

We don't see each other every day because we live far away.

The girls on talk on the phone and text but that's not enough,

Long distant relationships are tough.

Even though we can't see each other every day,

When we do get together we don't let that time pass.

We use every bit of it because that time won't last.

Too Good To Be True

You are too good for me as anyone could see.
How could I repay you for all of the things you do?
There was a time that I overacted,
Never once did you get distracted.
I enjoy the time we spend together,
No matter the weather
You stayed in my heart when I wanted to be Apart.
Throughout all of my ups and down,
You always stayed around.
Every time we touch, I love the feeling so much.
When we share a kiss, I could not resist.
My Past Relationships, always made me sad
But with you, I'm always glad.

It's Not That Serious

A stressed young girl whom seems think everything
Is going wrong in the world. Each and every day,
Instead of getting on her knees to pray. She
Overdose on drugs and alcohol hoping to
Get rid of it all.

Thru many years, she was stressed, depressed,
And cried so many tears. She couldn't take the pain
Any longer, though she wanted to get stronger.

She was alone with nobody around to help lift her
Off the ground. Since she felt no love nobody by
Her side, she kept doing drugs, than later she died.

Please Don't Go

My Darling Wife, the Love of my life, please don't go,
There's something you should know, and it's true,
I love you throughout everything we've been through.

We've been there for each other throughout all of our
Ups and downs, even when our family was pushed
On the ground.

I will accept my punishment of course, but please
Don't give me a divorce. Baby I'm on my knees, don't go
Please.

I've made a onetime mistake, but when I started
To feel bad, it was too late. I've betrayed our family
In the worse way I ever had.

The Right Choice

The day I first saw your face I wanted you in my space.
The first few weeks we talked and I was playing hard
To get. The feelings I had while in your arms, I shall never
Forget. When we're not together, I think about you
All of the time.

Every thought of you makes me feel jitters down my spine
Every time I kiss your lips, I feel passion through my body,
From my fingertips, down to my hips.

Each time I talk about us,
It sounds like a fairytale from a storybook.
As anyone could see, I was meant for you,
And you are meant for me. In love is where we were
Made to be. If you promise we'll Always be together,
I'll promise to love you forever.

I'm Not My Mother

A lot of people says "we are alike". I say "that's not
True". I don't do everything she do. We are the opposite.
Why is that so hard for some people to get?

She is my momma; we didn't come from the same vagina.
We're nothing like alike and for people to say that isn't right.
She drinks beer and smoke. I drink vodka and coke. One
Of us is sleep while the other is woke
Some things that I don't eat, to her, it's a tasty treat
And some things she don't like, I like them best.

We like different things, so we aren't as much alike
As it may seem.

Always Falling

For as long as I remember, that's all I do.
If I don't fall down, than I always trip,
Especially when I'm trying to sit.

Sometimes it's funny. Sometimes it's not.
Most of the time, I can laugh about it, but when
It hurts, I don't laugh @ all.

But falling down, It's always funny until someone
Gets hurt or maybe it's just me being overly silly.
I can even be walking down the street
And trip over my own feet.

Family

It's the second most important thing in the world.
It's more than just being Related, family should
Be together, the way GOD made it.

There are many different families. All share
One kind of love. Some shown in a different way.
But loves each other more and more every day.

Some families live near, others live far. Family should
Always love and care for one anther no matter how
Far apart they are, family should be sacred, whole,
Purified, most of all; saved by GOD

I tried to save my family, I really tried. Now all I could
Do is keep my feelings inside and rejoice because
Jesus is by my side.

I Want Peace

I want the war to end, but where do I begin. I try
To do Right, but temptation Always Attacks me everyday
And night, but my Reaction turns to sin. I tried to
Compromise, but she chose otherwise and I'm not surprised.

We have been in a war before sometime I feel like
I'm trapped behind a locked door. This war has
Been going on for years, I'm so tired of crying tears.

No matter what I do, I just can't get my mind @ ease.
Can I get some peace, please?

Good People

The way this rate is going, you'd think that the world
Is filled with a lot of Bad people. There's a lot of
Good people too. They just choose the Right things to do.

They are the people whom like to help others without
Expecting something back. Good people don't judge
Nor criticize other people no matter what they'll
Say or do, they would help you take care of you.

Sheba

Sheba was a wonderful pet. She never barked
Much, but I loved to feel that puppy Love touch.
She was light Brown and always played around.
I loved her and she loved me, she was my puppy.

One day, Late @ night, while I was in bed, tucked
In tight, I heard a bark. I Looked outside And
Saw nothing because it was dark. The next day
When I gave her food, There was no
Response, I wondered where could she be.
Then I found A neighbor came into my
Backyard and took her from me.

Oreo

He wasn't that bad of a cat. He had only one fault;
He kept peeing around the house, for some reason
He didn't wanna use his litter box except to poop.

Aside from that, we never saw a mouse in the house.
We didn't know why he had a weak bladder.
We did know that it stank.

We scrubbed and mopped everywhere, but still we
Smelled the scent through our nose hair.
We didn't open the door and just let him
Run away. We let him go the Right way
And gave him to the S.P.C.A.

Accept Your Own Advice "Never Say Can't"...

Is what I Always tell my Son, and never let it be told
To him by anyone; not even me. I left school because of bullies
And felt like a fool and that wasn't cool.

So I decided to get my G.E.D. instead, but the
Answers just wouldn't get in my head. I gave up
And it's been years.

A small voice then said into my ears, "Stop being a
Hypocrite, GO take your G.E.D. again, and
This time, you better not quit!

So I paid for the G.E.D. test and once again
I failed, it wasn't working out, after seeing
The results, all I can do is cry or pout.

After I was done, I sat down in deep thought about
How to come up with a different opportunity to
Succeed for myself and my family.

So I called the school district, they told me about
A high school diploma program called E.O.P.
I was glad and excited that it wasn't too late for me.

Apple Tree

I never saw an Apple Tree in the city, but on this
Day as I was on my way home, I saw an Apple
Tree. It looked good, I must admit, so I had to taste it.

The Apples wasn't on a big tree, but it was too
High from me. A young boy climbed the tree
And gave me one, than I asked him if he could
Get one for my son.

We took the Apples home and washed them off, than
Took a bite. They tasted so sweet and ripe,
Juicy and crunchy.

They tasted better than the Apples @ the
Supermarket. Those apples I would never forget.

It Ain't Easy

I don't get enough money. Just a little bit to
Try to get by, Sometimes that isn't enough,
Not being able to work is tough.

I'm on a fixed income, sometimes I wonder
When I'll be able to spend some.

I have a child, whom depends on me.
Sometimes I can't depend on myself
Because I don't have enough money.

I have plans to save money, but when I have
The chance, I always have to do something new.

I cry @ Night because I don't feel Right.
Not only I can't take care of me, but I can't
Take care of my family.

Go Away

In the beginning I thought you were cool,
Now you're making me look like a fool.

Now I feel like an Ass, because I thought
You had some class.

You Ain't Nobody except someone whom trying
To tear Apart my home. So leave me alone.
You go your way and I'll go my own.

A Good Man

A good man is hard to find.
Sometimes I wonder
"When will I find mine?"

Most of the good men whom I Discover
Belongs to another.
There were time I thought I had a good man,
But when I told him how I felt, he
Just got up and ran.

I don't let anyone get too close to my heart,
Because I don't want it ripped Apart.
I've been hurt so much I'm afraid to commit.

Some People don't understand why
I pull away my hand. Others think I'm being mean,
But it isn't as bad as
It may seem. I just can't find a good man.

To The Top

Climbing up the mountain without being able to see
What's @ the top in stored for me?
When I find a way up, I always fall down. I don't have the
Strength to get off the ground.

It's really hard, I don't think I'm gonna make it,
But I need to be it's too late. I want scrape all of
My troubles off my plate, and walk through
The golden gate.

Justice

Justice number one; she was a lot of fun. We walked,
Ran, and played in the park and always in the house
Before it gets dark, I loved her with all of my heart.
She was a really good friend until the End. Then I
Found out she was sick; that she wouldn't
Catch another stick. Later, she died and
I felt bad inside.

Justice number two; we had so much to do.
We had a lot of fun. He did much more than
Just bark and run; he enjoyed bathing in the sun.
When I relaxed while watching TV, he was always
With me. As I was sleeping, he was doing the
Same. He was obedient and always came when we
Called his name. He was more than just a great pet,
He was great entertainment and that we'll never
Forget.

Both Dogs were well trained, we never complained.
They were always in a good mood and never rude.
When a few children were afraid we showed them
They were friendly and then they played.
They never chased a cat; imagine that.

Philadelphia

A city where I was born and raised.
A place where there's a lot of good and bad days.
If people stop the violence and keep it clean,
Our city won't be as bad as it may seem.

Our City is beautiful. I'd stay that way if
People stop littering and killing every day.
Philadelphia has many sights to see.
You can visit alone or better with your family.

We have Penn's Landing, Liacouras Center, and Civic
Center, casinos, theaters, hotels, statues, malls,
Museums, buildings over 100 ft. tall. I wish I
Could see them all. This is just a few. There
Are many things to do? We even have the
Philadelphia Zoo.

Sometimes I like to go outside just to roam and
Enjoy the smell of Nature's fresh Air. I may
Say I'm moving out of Philadelphia. I love it
Here, I'm not going anywhere.
Philadelphia, is my Home where I belong.

Queen Mom

Mother of our family tree, I wish you were still
Here with me. Our family would be a mess,
If you didn't teach us how to Love and what
We know best.

I never felt so loved by anyone except the Love I
Have from GOD. You never judged nor criticized.
Everyone turned to you when a problem needed
To be solved, you always knew when to get involved.

On your face have always been a smile
Because that was your style. No matter what went
Down you never frowned.

Grandma I miss you. I know you're now living
With GOD, but I miss being by your side,
I need you here too. It still hurts today
That I remember the day you went away.

Christmas Day

It's much more than receiving and giving gifts
Away. It's all about praising and worshiping GOD for
Jesus being born on this day.

Later in life; He was nailed to the cross and crucified
Than he died; three days later, he arose again.

Before we came out of the womb, Jesus Christ knew us
Before we knew him. We praise, worship, and love
Him because he first loved us.

I Want To Be Loved

Why don't you love me? I love you
My love for you is real, unconditional, and true.
I'll always love you no matter what we go through.
When we shared our first kiss, I knew it was right.
I think about you every day and night. I miss
You so much whenever you're out of my sight.

I'm so happy with you in my life. I was hoping
Someday I'll become your wife, but now I see it'll
Never come true because you don't feel about me
The way I feel about you. I thought it takes two
People to be in a Relationship,
But it feels like it's only one and it's no fun.

I wanted our Relationship to develop into something
More and lasts for years instead I feel sad and
Cry tears. I thought we'd be together forever.
My feelings for you are true and it's hard to hide
Inside. Can you blame me for wanting you by my side?
Why don't you love me? I Love you so much, but I
Need more than your sexual touch. You have my
Whole heart and nobody else do. You know I'm
Willing to do any and everything for you, but on
One condition, you have to Love me too.

I'm Going Home

No more tears, no more fears.
Don't cry because I'm no longer here.

Smile, because GOD has another plan for me.
I'm going home where I'm supposed to be.

It's devastating with everyone I leave behind.
My body may be gone, but in your hearts, we're
Always together, because I live forever.

Love Or Lust

Nobody could possibly imagine the way my
Hormones are going through me right now.
It might be love, it could be lust. I don't know
How I feel but I do know my feelings are real.

Whenever I think about him I feel all tingly inside
Yet; I don't tell him how I feel because
I have too much pride.

Somehow and some way I will tell him one day
This is a game that I Don't
Know how to play.

Get Out

Get out, you shouldn't be here. You cause
Everyone to stress, your life is just one big mess.
If nobody wanted me around. I would've been
Out of town.

You caused our family to get sick. They shouldn't
Have to scream and shout because of you
So get out. It's a shame, you don't even care
And think this is all just a game. Since you feel
That way. Pack your things and get out of here.

A Closed Mouth

It's been Always told for many years
"A closed mouth won't get fed." That Quote is so true.
If you love someone you should tell them how
You feel and keep it real.

Some People holds in their feelings for a very long
Time, but when they finally found the courage
To say anything it'll be too late.

Than you start to feel bad, because you lost the
Most important person in your life you ever had.

Happy Birthday

Happy Birthday to you. Nobody can Love you
The way we do. Today should be the joyous day
Of your life and Avoid any strife.

Celebrate today because it belongs to you.
If you have any friends, let them celebrate too.

Running Water

What is happening? Why is there so much?
It's too much water spilled from one drink.
Something is really wrong, maybe, it's
Just the plumbing. It's not working right,
The water runs all day and night.

It's frustrating dealing with this every day.
Whenever I handled the situation, or so I thought;
It's not doing any good. So as I should, I have
To handle it in a different way.

Nights Of Passion

If two people wants to be together; the Passion begins.
If they Love each other; the Passion never ends.
Passion for one night; always feels right.

Making you wanting more, it's so tense, Nobody minds
Hitting the floor, and don't care if the
Neighbors hear from next door.

A Mother's Nightmare

WTF!! Is going on here? My suspicions better
Be a nightmare, or else nobody's going anywhere
I gave my child to you and this is what you do?
My Baby says something happened, so I wanna know
What!! My child wouldn't lie, if it wasn't true,
Why would my baby cry?

How come my child's afraid of my motherly touch?
Which used to be loved so much. I'm so stressed out.
Mixed emotions everywhere inside of me.

I have a lot of fears. I can't stop crying so many tears.
I need to find a way to get my mind @ ease
To do so, I'll call the police. Someone take
My fears away please.

My Way

It's my way or no way @ all. When someone tells me
What to do and I don't approve it won't get done.
I'm stubborn, as any person could see, sometime I
Care about nobody but me.

I also can be selfish too. Half the time, I won't admit
That it's true. When I have an attitude I can be very rude
And not care what anyone say until things
Will go my way.

What Would You Do?

What would you do? If someone says "they
Can raise your child better than you?"

How would you feel, if someone says
"That you love isn't real?"

Which expression will you have on your face,
Knowing someone is trying to take your place?

Where is the pain you feel deep in your heart
When you find out others are trying
To tear you apart?

Who will you run to when you feel lost and
Don't know what else to do?

Why beat yourself up with all of these Questions?

The answer is simple; Go to GOD,
Sit down and pray. Tell Jesus all about your day
He'll show you the way.

When you're not feeling Right, call upon Jesus,
He'll never steer you wrong. He's available
24/7 and he'll listen to you all day long.

Again I Tried

Today I took the Math Part of my G.E.D. My Diploma
Means so much to me. Before I leave this world,
I wanna be able to tell myself "you GO Girl".
But I won't know until the results come back.

I hope I passed because today I want it to be the last
So today I received my results and there's
And there's no surprise that I did not pass.

What is it about this test that has my brain @ rest?
I studied @ home, even went to G.E.D. class,
But yet, I still can't pass.

Not Now, but one day, I will try Again
And I'm gonna keep on trying until the very end.

Zodiac Signs

Who would've thought that a bull could have
Great sex with a goat and make that little
Goat wanting more.

That little goat must like to dominate, Rough,
Hardcore sex and loves to sweat because
The bull likes to take control.

The goat likes to take control sometimes too,
And they're good @ what they do.
Mixed breed Signs can have their fun too,
Not just those of their own kind.

A Friend In Jesus

When you're feeling down, sad, and blue,
Call upon Jesus; he'll take good care of you.
When you feel all hope is gone, just remember
You're never alone.

If you're in trouble, he'll be there on the double.
When you need someone to talk to, tell it to Jesus,
He'll listen to you

Get on your knees and pray, he hears you every night
And day, he'll be with you all the way.
Just believe in him and you'll be alright.

Even if you don't go to church, continue
Living Right and put him first, As long As
You keep the faith and know what he's worth.

Our father, which art in heaven, hollowed be thy
NAME. Thou Kingdom come, thou will be done.
On Earth, as it is in heaven. Give us this day,
Our daily bread, and forgive us our trespasses,
As we forgive those who trespassed against us.
And lead us not, into temptations, but deliver us
From Evil. For thy is the kingdom, the power,
The glory, forever, AMEN.

Halloween

Halloween; what is it? Sounds like hypocrisy
To me. Did we forget what was taught by our family?

We were taught "Not to talk to strangers," "Not to go
With strangers," and most of all "not to accept
Anything from strangers".

But yet, we allow our children to knock on strangers'
Doors and ask them for candy.

Haven't we watched the news or somehow,
Did we all just got confused?

Children become missing every day, from homes,
Schools, even from around the way.

What if (GOD forbid) children don't come?
Back home where they belong?

What are they going "trick-or-treating" for?
Why not buy candy from the store?
And most people don't like others
Knocking @ their doors.

Momma's Boy

He'll always be my baby boy, and there's no maybe,
He's handsome, loving, and smart. He'll always
Have my heart, he had it from the start.

He's young now, but when he gets old,
Still he won't be able to break
Mommas tight hold, it'll get even tighter
When it's cold.

Scared

Today was the worse! I never knew I could be so scared
They way kids play is so weird. I also was angry
But I didn't curse.

Thank you Lord for being there for my baby. It
Wouldn't have happened if he was right
Next to me.

With so many thoughts running through my mind,
I can't even think right. Thank you GOD for
Holding him tight. I don't know what I'll
Do if I couldn't watch him sleep @ night

Lose Weight Gain

Man!! This is really getting on my nerves.
I can hardly see my curves.

Every time I lose some weight I gain more.
My Butt's so big, I almost can't fit through the door.

Sometimes I just feel like giving up, because
Trying to lose this weight is tough.

I often exercise, I even changed the way and
Portions I eat my food. Dieting and exercising
Is a waste of my time, because it's doing
No good for my waistline.

People always throw it in my face, especially when
It's not their place. I know my weight is in the way.
I deal with it every day. I try to lose it,
But then it'll come back and stay.

Anything For You

I don't know why I feel this way, but it's true,
That I will do anything for you. As many times
I could tell you "no", I'll end up doing it anyways.
I guess it's because I don't wanna let you down,
But always keep you around.

Anytime, Any Place, Anywhere, whenever you want me,
I'm there. If you wanted me to; I'd lick you
From your neck to your feet, what a tasteful treat.

The First Day

I remember the first day my baby went off
To go to school. He enjoys learning more and more
Every day in his very own way.

Not only that I chose the Right school,
But his teachers are very cool. They never beat
Around the bush, but always keeps it Real.
And let me know what's the deal.

I also like his principal. She always wears a smile
And she really cares. I wish there were
More people like her everywhere.

My First Baby

My first baby, I can't wait. Feeling the movement
In my belly every day and night makes me more
Anxious to hold my baby tight.

Now the day has come, that I can hold and
Breastfeed my little one, with hair so soft,
Skin so smooth and such a beautiful face,
No other child can take my Baby's place.

My first baby means, it's my turn to be a mom.
No more parting and wasting my time
Because it's no longer mine.
So now I say goodbye to relaxing and sleeping
Peacefully now that I have my own family.

Far And Near

Although you are far away, your love is always near,
And I will always be here because
I'm not going nowhere.

It was always told that "Long distant Relationships
Won't work" out, but we'll find out what
That's all about, and if it's true, than I wasn't
Meant to be with you.

We may not be able to see each other every day,
But we can send pictures and write to
Make us feel better. There's no need to cry,
I will be home soon. We will be a family again.

Let Them Be Kids

All children are special and are precious gifts.
So let them be kids, see them learn, laugh and play,
Love them more and more every day.

Encourage and believe in their hope and dreams.
Never put down their self-esteems. Understand
Their knowledge, acknowledge their skills.
Teach them right from wrong provide good food
So they can eat smart to grow up big and strong.

Don't force nor push them to grow up so fast.
Let them be kids while the time last,
So when they do grow up, there will be no regret
Letting that time past.

Invisible Mother

On August 2, 2008, I gave birth to a
Handsome, healthy, baby boy. I thought my
Life will be filled with so much joy.

It ain't as easy as I thought it would be,
But I wanted this to be my opportunity
To be a parent and live happily.

I know there's others whom loves him
Just as much as I do, but the need
To let his mother through,

I want a chance to live life with my son,
He's my only one. It feels like my life as a parent
Has come to an end, because instead
Of his mother, I feel more so of his
Sister and friend.

Out Of Control

What should I do? I can't take no more!!
Hollering, Screaming, while stomping on the floor.

Talking back to me every day, not listening
And doing what I say. I'm dealing with
And out of control little boy, who plays with
Me as if I'm a little toy.

I tried punishment and spankings, but that's
Not enough and @ the same time,
I don't wanna get too rough.

I'm not trying to give my baby a black eye.
I also don't want to hurt him too much
Because I really don't like to see him cry.

A New Baby

Today is finally here. We waited nine months
For this special day to come.

All of those times seeing the baby through an
Ultrasound, now being a parent will
Turn my life around.

It never matted to me, if the baby, was a boy or girl.
I just knew he or she would change my world.

What If?

I know GOD says…"obey your mother and
Father, than your days will be longer here
On Earth", but…

What if your parents put you down, calls you
Names, no longer wants you around, and beats
You until you fall to the ground?

What if there isn't a day that goes by they don't
Scream and shout, make false accusations, gossip,
And threatens to kick you out?

What if in your younger days, you were taken
Advantage of, in so many ways, and nobody showed
You any love?

Now, what is it to do then? Do you stay and let the
Abuser win? Do you still stay, take the abuse,
And obey? Or do you pack your things
And run away? What if this has happened to you?
What would you do?

The Perfect Day

The Perfect Day...is when children
Can go outside and play.

The Perfect Day...is clear skies, sun shining so
Bright, nice cool breeze until it turns night.
The Perfect Day...is not too hot, it's not too cold,
No stormy rain, but a little drizzle. I Don't
Like hot nor cold weather, but just in the middle.

The Perfect Day...is all sirens are silenced
And the news doesn't mention one act of violence.
That's my idea of the Perfect Day.

Kissing You

Feeling your lips gently against mine, Feeling like I'm
Kissing a cloud. Smooth, fluffy, soft lips, got me
Feeling sexual healing all through my hips.

Kissing you makes me feel so good. It makes me feel
Like a woman should. The way you kiss me makes me
Feel free. As anyone can see, you and I were meant to be.

Kissing you makes my heart beat more faster
Even I could feel it pounding against my chest,
Kissing you is the best.

Skin Deep

There's a Quote that states "Beauty is skin Deep",
But if that's so, than how come most
Women wear make-up?

Women should accept and be proud of the skin
They were born in. Why not like the skin you're in?
Instead of wearing make-up and making your skin torn

All is needed is some lotion to soften and moisturize
Your skin, and why get a tan. Because you think your
Skin is too bright? Most of them are dangerous and
Your skin won't turn out Right.

Sexual Feelings

My body knows what it wants. I'm gonna
Make sure it gets it. When I'm in the shower,
I stay in there for @least an hour.

Feeling the water running down my body
Really gets me in the mood. Especially when
It runs from my head to my feet
Make me weak.

Privacy Please

I need my own space. Why are people always
In my face. Gossiping about me, when it
Isn't their place.

Why worry about where I been? What I'm doing?
Where I'm going? Can I have my privacy?
I'm gonna do me Regardless how you
Want me to be.

Stay out of my room and out of my things,
Stop eaves dropping on my calls just because
You heard the rings.

Don't worry about where I am or the places
I want to go. Some things isn't your business
And you shouldn't know.
I'll feel more @ ease, if you just
Give me privacy please!

On My Mind

It's been many years, you stayed on my mind
All of the time. There are things to know that
I should've let go.

I remember how many time and where we started
Our passionate moments. It's shocking some
Feelings are still there.

Isn't it a shame that I remember your birthday,
Age, first and last name? For me to still know
All of this, I must be insane.

As you can see; I'll never forget my first. I Always
Asked myself "what will I do if I ever saw
You? I was so shocked and amazed,
My head was about to burst.

The Brothers

The two brothers, one Love their mother more
Than the other.

He showers his mother with candy and flowers, while
The other won't even give her a dollar,

One of the two brothers is Rich with no family,
While the other is married with children
And still gives as much love as he can.

Every day, he buys her Diamonds, pearls, silver, and Gold
While the other brother can't wait until she gets old.

Reunited

It's so good to see you again after so long.
Now that I have, I want more than to be your friend.

I wasn't us to pick up where we left off and
This time make it even better than the last.

We ain't getting no younger and the days
Are going by very fast.

I don't know how to begin to describe how
I feel knowing this is real and true.

I have another chance to be with you
And you to be with me too

Thanksgiving Day

A traditional family dinner that's usually
Shared once a year. This is a day to bond
With one another, appreciate the things we have
And the people to show love with everyone
We know.

Some families enjoy getting together to have
Fun and to talk about different things
Others wanna come around when the food get
Done, sit around and fight, but good cooking
And good eating always make things Right.

Stolen Life

A baby boy whose life filled with so much joy,
Until one day he tried to run away, when he was
A teen, but his life didn't turn out as good as it seemed.

He was kidnapped by a group of thugs, all he wanted
Was a few hugs. He got kicked around until he fell
To the ground, than hid him from the world,
So he wouldn't be found.

As he grew from a boy to a man, he still didn't
Understand, when he learned the truth, he ran
Found his way back home, though, he felt he was still alone.

So Cruel

I feel disrespected. How can they even think my children
Were neglected? They are my Babies, I'm their
Mother and there is no other.

I carried them in my Belly, went to the Doctor's every week,
Took more medication every day, than they were on the way.

Those were the best experiences in my whole life.
Why would you think I would destroy theirs? I love them
With all of my heart, mind, body, and soul. There's
Nothing I wouldn't do for my babies, no if's Ands, but's
About it nor maybe.

They're part of me and forever will be. Now the thought
Of someone to think I would hurt them,
Now that's cold

Is He Really Here?

I know he's alive,
I know he's there,
But I can't feel him anywhere

Miraculous things happen every day and every night.
How can I believe in him
When he's not in my sight?

A New Year is coming.
It's time for a new way
To get him into my heart.

I have faith, but I need more.
Since I don't feel him inside,
How do I know he's by my side?

When I do go to church, I feel like a hypocrite,
Though, I go to hear the word and feel the spirit,
Sometimes I'm ashamed to go there
Because I don't know if he's really here,
Because I don't feel him anywhere.

Insecurity

As a teen, can't nobody tell me a thing?
I was beautiful with a nice body.
I was proud to be me.
Now I feel and think I look fat.
Some People agree with me,
Others think I'm crazy.

I'm beautiful and I want my beautiful body back,
So I could wear the clothes I used to wear
And no longer have to be Ashamed or
Embarrassed to go out to the mall
And stores for shopping.

I diet and exercise to try to lose this weight,
So I can feel great, because I have no energy,
All of this weight is sucking it out of me.

Of all of this work, I'd thought I'd have a lot
Of progress, but I don't, so I won't and I
Don't care because it don't look like
This weight isn't going anywhere.

Peer Pressure

Peer Pressure hurts, more than anything physical.
Those whom pressuring thinks it's a game,
But those whom being pressured
Feels a lot of shame.

Some get over it and others don't because
They have a lot of Regret @ the End.
Those whom you thought were your
Friends wasn't being a very good friend.

It can really bring down someone's
Self-esteem. Some people thinks
It's no big deal, but they don't know
How it feels.

Peer Pressure is not only cruel, but it's
Rude, especially when it happens
In front of others.

I don't see how people could
Be so mean and do it for fun,
Not thinking it's hurting anyone.

Could It Be?

Could it be? I've finally met the man
Whom is right for me? My empty cup
Is now filling up. Of all these years,
I can now stop crying tears.

For many years, I've been rejected.
It happened so much I now expect it,
But I'd often walk way before
I started to feel neglected.
Could it be? For once, in a relationship
I'd finally get respected?

This is too good to be true. I'd have
To stay in this relationship longer
To see if it will grow stronger.

His kiss, I can't resist, when I'm cold,
He squeezes me in a tight hold.
When we're together, he makes me feel
Good just as a woman should.
I wish I can be held like this forever.

In My Life Again

In the Past, when we were together
I though our relationship would last.
I loved you, I thought you loved me too.

You really broke my heart. Then I
Realized you didn't care @ all. You didn't
Even bother to give me a call.

I cried so many tears. Now I see you
Again after so many years, I wanna
Start over, but can I trust you not to
Let me down? Because I wanna be more
Than just your friend.

Sometimes I daydream about us being
Together. You caressing me while we kiss
About to get undressed, than someone
Snaps me back into reality.
Well, I don't wanna daydream anymore
I want to be with you and you to
Be with me too.

I Want You Back

Throughout all of the drama and arguing
We had, I pushed you away because
I was mad. Now that you been gone
For so long, I'm now feeling very sad.

I miss you and I hope you miss me too.
I want you to come back home
Where you belong.

Will you come back home to me, if I
Promise to love unconditionally?
We need you to stay home for our family.

I think about us every night, wondering how
I could make it Right, I know I told
You to leave us alone, but now I feel so
Weak that I'm too ashamed to speak.

I'm so stressed and depressed, it's having
A bad effect on my life. I want us to
Have a new start to be in each other's
Heart.

Beautiful Eyes

Whenever I look @ you I start to smile
Because I notice you looking back @ me.

Seeing the sparkle in your eyes reminds me of
The stars in the midnight blue skies and
They're bright like the morning sunrise.

They're so big and perfectly round, I look
At you all day if nothing else gets in my way.

If it were up to me, I'd look into your beautiful eyes
24/7, it feels so dreamy looking into your eyes
Is like looking into heaven.

It's Not Right

It isn't Right for the closings of schools,
They must want kids to feel like fools.

What are we to do to stop this process
From going through?

Where will all the children go? If they
Decide to do so? I would like to see
Children succeed, especially for those
Whom yet haven't learned how to read?

You have your education, why not let these
Children have one too?

Everyone wants a career, but with you closing
Down schools, it isn't Right and isn't fair.

No Heat

In the beginning of spring, doesn't mean a thing.
In the house, there isn't any gas.
So the warmth didn't last.

In there lives a large family and it's just as
Cold as it can be. It's warmer outside than it is
In here. There's no hot water to take a shower
It's getting colder by the hour.

We can't use the stove to boil some water
Because the stove is gas too. Neither of us
Knows what to do.

Mother's Day

A day for all of the women and mother,
Mother mind the brother.

This is a day just for us and for the men to
Express their love and show they care,
By taking us anywhere.

Though it should be cherished everyday,
Mother's day only come once a year.

Fuel To The Fire

A middle-age girl feels like everything is going
Wrong in her world. She tried to live Right
Every day, but people keep attacking her in
Each and every way.

She tried to keep her head up high, but
Negativity always comes by. The girl don't like
To be mean, most of the time, she's like a ball of
Fire and people add fuel until she blows up
Now everybody think she's a fool and just
Being cruel.

Everyone Assumes she's "the bad Guy" and
Nobody knows the reason why. If people continue
To add "fuel to the fire" someone
Eventually will get burned, they know the lesson,
But still haven't learned.

My Sweet Valentine

Dear Sweet Valentine, I wish you were mine
I miss feeling your soft lips caressing and
Kissing me from my neck to my hips.

Tonight I want to drop the rose pedals,
Pour the wine, light scented candles, and dance
All night until the mood is right.

Since the first day, I never wanted you to go
Away. I thought we'd always be together forever
What I miss most is us holding each other close.

If I had one last chance, to make a wish,
It'll be a night of Romance, so I can remember
And cherish our love shared and the one
And only last dance.

Let It Snow

In the months of November and December, There
Were no snow @ all, but in January and February
Than it starts to fall.

After it's done, the snow on the ground look a lot of fun
But it ain't so nice slipping and sliding on ice. Not all
Snow is that bad. Some make children happy from sad,
It's soft and mushy with crystals all around.

Snow is cold and it doesn't get old. We always have to
Bundle so we could stay warm. Up in the mountains where there
Is a lot of snow people like skiing and skating and riding
On the sled hoping not to bang their head.

I'm Sorry

I'm sorry I've hurt you
And for all of the stress
I've put you through.

Please forgive me, for I didn't know
I was confident in my heart
He belonged to you.

Because of this serious mistake,
You turned your back and walked away,
But now I'm begging for you to stay.

I'm on my hands and knees,
Crying my every tear,
Hoping you forgive me and come back here.

If there's anything you want me to do,
I'm willing to make it up to you.
I would not say "no" because I don't want you to go.

Please forgive me,
And come back home.
I don't want to be alone. I'm sorry.

Am I Good?

I try to be a good mom. I try to be smart
About it too, but when times get hard
Sometimes I don't even know what to do.

I'm always around no matter what goes down.
When times are happy or sad, whether their
Behavior is good or bad. Especially when they
Get mad and their precious faces turns
Into a frown.

I make sure they get to school, so they won't
Grow up to be a fool, when they get sick, I make
Sure they see a doctor quick.

Sometimes I feel like my mind wanders off track
But I'll never turn my back, and from time to time,
I always asks myself...Am I Being a good mom?

My Little Kittens

My little kittens, so cute and so small.
Their eyes still closed and only two inches tall.

The kittens have soft and smooth fur. I like
To hear their little purr with their four
Tiny paws and could barely crawl.

They don't yet have a voice box, so only a
Mother can hear their call, but it's adorable to
See them try to let out their little cry.

One More Chance

Please forgive me, for what I said isn't true.
I really do love you. I think of you within every
Beat of my heart. I knew we were meant for each
Other right from the start.

I regret the thing I have said while I was
Speaking from my head. I will miss you too much if
You're not here so I can feel your tender touch, when
I kiss your lips and your hands caressing my hips.

Please don't go I want our love to have the chance
To grow and someday, have our own family no matter
What you do; please don't leave me.

If You Were Mine

If you were mine, I'll be with you all of the
Time and make sure you feel fine.

If you belonged to me, I'll let you see, that
We were meant to be.

If we were to be together, my love would
Last forever.

If you were my girl, I'd give you the world.

If I were your man, I'd give you my hand and
Make you understand, I'd give you all of my
Time, if you were mine.

Why Now?

All the while, you have the chance, you never
Have been around. Now that I'm with someone
Else, you try to turn my relationship upside down.

You tell me "you love me and we should be
Together for our family tree, and the feeling
You have are real." But you're too late.
Ever being with you was a mistake.

Why now? You decide to care, when I have
No more love to share, and I'm going with you
Nowhere. You need to understand that I have
A new man, in my life, hopefully one day
I'll become his wife.

So, why now? After all the while you left town.
Do what you do best and go away. I don't wanna
See you another day.

Tears Of Love

Every day and night, as I think about you, tears are
Falling from my eyes. Now this is a surprise.
This has never happened to me before
Until now, that I think of someone than start to
Cry and I don't know why.

When I want to see you, but I can't get through
I start to cry than too, but when I can I don't
Know what to do. Sometimes I imagine me bring held in
Your arms and I smile wide as the sea. Then I cry
When I realize it was just me.

Every time I See You

Every time I see you, I wanna kiss your lips, while your
Hands caressing my hips

Every time I see you, lying there in bed. I lie down
Next to you resting my head on your chest, well
You know the rest.

Every time I see you, step into the shower, I'd get in
With you and we'll be @ least an hour.

Every time I see you, in the winter time when you
Come around, you make the snow and ice melt
Because you're so hot, you really know
To hit the spot.

Every time I see you, I'm a loss for words because
I don't know what to say or do.

Take Me Home

Please don't cry. I'm just going to my home in the sky.

While I was here, I was suffering with so much pain.
I had no more strength for me to gain.

Now that I'll be living with GOD, I know he'll be
Right by my side.

Stop the falling tears, we had many good years
But I'm just going home. Don't worry, I won't
Be alone.

In Love Alone

A beautiful couple been together for many years.
He finally asked for her hand in marriage, but
She didn't want to deal with that much baggage.

So, she refused, than he felt he was just being
Used and verbally abused. So, he left for one week,
When she saw him, she didn't even speak.

He moved back in he asked her again, she said
"No, you gotta go, and I don't wanna be your friend!"
And that's the end.

Can't Hide Love

Two young children whom laughed and played
All day long, grew up liking each other more,
Than ready to explore.

When they have grown, they broke apart to be on
Their own. All the while they were gone, each one
Feeling alone.

They tried dating to replace the empty space they have
In their hearts.

They found love, but wasn't in it. Neither both of them
Couldn't win it, but then they found each other.
Neither wants to be away from the other, so
They got married and lived happily with
Their family.

The Way I Feel

I don't know these feeling that I feel. Whether
Its love or lust, but I do know that they are real.

I often try to hide these feeling inside. I won't
Allow them to show because I have too much pride.

The way I feel every time I see your face, when you
Go away the vision of seeing you can never be erased.

Busted

An escape ex-convict taking advantage of people because
They're sick. Every day he's robbing homes and
Breaking into cars. He even stole money from A
Few bars. He don't have a partner, because he like to
Work alone.

One day he tried to rob a bank, but he didn't think about
The security cameras everywhere, but then he tried to
Get out of there when a police officer said
"Freeze" he then dropped to his knees.

Should We Be Together?

If the feelings are real honest and true, than what else
Is there to do? We feel the deep in our heart, but
Something always gets in the way and tear us apart.

After a while, we're together again. Most people say
We'd make a good couple, but what do we think of each other
Should we be together?

It's You

It's you, the one whom have been in my thoughts
And dreams. I guess being with you won't be so
Bad as it may seems.

It's you, the one I want to be with for life and
Maybe someday I'll be your wide.

It's you whom I supposed to be with to keep our
Family together, hoping our love will last forever.

I love to see your smile and the glare in your eyes.
Every time I see you, it's always a surprise.

It's you, I think of every night, wanting you next
To me holding each other tight.

It's you, whom always in my heart, the one I always
Loved from the start.

Trapped

Just because I have a few babies, I didn't know
I was saying goodbye to my life.

I can't go out @ all, not even to the mall.
I want to have fun, get my hair, toes, and nails done,
Maybe even a facial wax too. Being in this house,
I have nothing to do.

The Way I feel

I don't know these feeling that I feel. Whether
Its love or lust, but I do know that they are real.

I often try to hide these feelings inside, I won't
Allow them to show because I have too much pride.

The way I feel every time I see your face, when you
Go away the vision of seeing you can never be erased.

Should We Be Together?

If the feelings are real honest and true, than what else
Is there to do? We feel the deep in our heart, but
Something always gets in the way and tear us apart.

After a while, we're together again. Most people say
We'd make a good couple, but what do we think of each other
Should we be together?

We Are Family

We're not blood, but we love each other
Very much as if we were, I'd do anything for you,
You'd do anything for me. We really do care
As anyone could see.

No matter where we are, whether we are
Near or far, we will always be family.
When you need me, if you're healthy or sick,
I'll be there for you quick.

When you're feeling low and choose to give
Me a call, I'll be there to catch you before you fall.
I know you'll do the same for me
Because we are family.

Night Of Passion

It's been so long since we last seen each other
So tonight I just want us to hold one anther
After holding each other tight, I want you to turn
Off the light, so we'll set the mood right because
I want you tonight.

It has been years that I've been crying tears
Because you've been on my mind all of the time,
It seems as if it was only yesterday you went away.

Now that you're here, I don't want you to go
Anywhere. I belong to you and you belong to me,
In your arms, is where I want to be.

I Want You

I want you, if only you knew how much I do.

I want us to be together "always and forever".

I want you, to have and to hold until we get old.

I want you, in the day and night, anytime will be Right.

I want you, to caress my boys, make love to me,
And start our own family.

Silent Tears

Alone in a room with nobody else there, sometimes I
Feel sad, than down come that first tear. Sometimes
I cry for hours, even days. My feelings change in so many ways.

Nobody will ever know about the feelings I hide inside,
They change like the weather and move like a Roller
Coaster Ride.

There are time when I think I may be depressed. I
Also thing I may be stressed, but crying is what I do
Most. I turn off the TV, Radio, and the light. Still I
Can't seem to get sleep @ night.

Everyday I'm feeling this way. I can't find a way out,
I'm still crying and don't know what my tears are about.

Undercover Lovers

A young couple married a very long time. She
Loved and trusted her husband, so his
"Working late" she didn't pay it no mind.

One late night, while in bed, she woke up scratching
Her head. Wondering who's knocking @ the door,
When it's a quarter after four? Another woman holds a
Baby in her hand, the wife was shocked and still
Didn't understand. She asked herself "Do this baby
Belong to my man?"

When her husband gotten home, the other line beeped
While he was on the phone; he found out his wife
Was having an affair of her own.

Moonlit Skies

Tonight, the stars and the moon are shinning so bright
Not as the sun, but a Dimmer one.

The sky is so beautiful, makes you wanna look up and
Stare @ the glare and don't wanna go anywhere.

A perfect moon lit sky, makes you wish you could fly.
Soaring up into the air while feeling the cool
Breeze blowing through your hair.

Lonely Memories

We have shared our good times, and our bad.
Whether they were happy or sad. I remember, them
All just if it was only yesterday. Now you are
Pushing me away. Without you, I feel so alone,
I wish you come back home, to be with me]
And have our own family.

I miss you, I miss seeing your face, I miss
Hearing your voice. I don't wanna let you go,
But I don't have a choice. Nobody else could
Ever take your place.

I like kissing your lips. I loved the way you
Caressed my hips. I want you in my life,
I feel so bad, because you were
The best lover I ever had.

# Butterfly

Oh! How I wish I were a butterfly. Soaring
Through the air without a care.

Oh! How I wish I were a butterfly.
Flying up so high in the sky, while gliding through
The clouds, free, to go anywhere, until down
Goes the sun, than my flying is done.

That's why I wish I were a butterfly.

Wanting More

My life is alright. I have a nice house, car,
And a good job too. So why can't I sleep
@ Night? Because I have nobody there to hold
And squeeze me tight.

I need more money. I'm not making enough. Sitting
Here crying because it's hard to get by and make
Ends meet I barely have anything to eat.

I'm living good, but not well, but only time will tell.
When I'll be able to get all of the things I need
And want, especially a husband, so he'll share his life
With me because that's the way it should be.

Working Out

I feel great, going to the gym and lose weight,
It takes the stress away and makes me feel
Good all day. I've gained confidence and
More self-esteem.

I also have more energy. I'm glad I'm going
This for me. Sometimes I feel hurt and pain
But it doesn't matter because I have a lot of
Strength that I've gained.

Forever Mine

We've been together for many years.
There were many times I cried, but you
Wiped away all of my tears. You gave me comfort
Throughout all of my fears.

During the time of struggle, you were there on
The double. You stood by my side when I was in
Trouble. When I was homeless, lying around, you
Took my hand and pulled me up from the ground.

You brought me to your home and said, "Here is
Where I belong and here is where I'll stay, so
We'll be together everyday."

Today we got married and soon to be working
On our family. I belong to you, you belong to me.
I'm forever yours and you're forever mine.

My Hero

One day I went to pick up my son (4 yrs.) from
School, than I got sick, that wasn't cool.

I'm very proud of my son for calling 911. I can
Never thank him enough, for my little man being
So tough.

I'm so glad I taught him how to dial my phone
In case we are alone.

Socks

She was black with white Paws. She had some
Really sharp claws. She was a cute and good
Little kitten, but turned out to be a bad cat.

She liked to play, but not every day. She attached
Anyone or thing in her way. If she saw a mouse,
She'd take it out and leave evidence behind.

I adored her until she got carried away.
She was biting, scratching up the baby,
Now that wasn't a maybe, she had to go.

There were times that I thought it wasn't
Her fault and she was provoked. I really wanted
Her back, but I didn't was to risk her
Scratching the baby again. I wasn't having that.

Feeling The Wind

Taking a nice long walk on this beautiful day,
With no heavy clouds coming my way.
Nice cool breeze blowing from the sky, going
Through my hair. I could walk just about anywhere.

It's so nice, I wanna ride my bike and fly a kite.
Today's weather is just Right. I don't want it
To become night.

M.Y.O.B.

I always voice my opinions, even though it has
Nothing to do with me, but it does involve my family.
I thought everyone was entitled to their own opinions.

Someone was about to smoke on the bus,
Then I started to fuss. So, I told the driver.
She saw a co-worker than called him over.

I told him who was the guy. He made it
Seem as though I told a lie. When he was
Approached, he told the driver "he wasn't
Trying to smoke".

When I got home, I told my parents and they
Both said to me "Girl, you better mind your
Own Business! People out here are crazy!!

Identity Theft

It really did mess up my life and turned it around.
It is as bad as it sound.

My credit is so bad, I can't even get a loan.
I'll never be able to buy my own home.

My life is so torn apart, I don't know where to start.
If only I knew, how to make it through, living so rough
I didn't think my life will be so tough.

All Alone

I once loved and cared for someone
Only to find out, that someone doesn't
Love me back. I think about her so much
My mind wanders and get off track.

I talk to everyone about her. Says "she's special to me",
But she doesn't feel the same way. I've
Tried telling her how I feel hoping she
Would keep it real.

I want to feel her warm hug and share a long,
Sweet, tender kiss that I just couldn't resist.
It hurts me so much to know, I'll never
Feel her passionate touch.

Goodbye

After all of these years of being together now
We separate. Now I'm sitting here, crying so many
Tears, being together for all of this time were
Great, who would ever think we'd be apart.
All of this time you were in my heart.

We now have jobs in different city. Sometimes
I wonder if you'd ever miss me. I'll definitely miss
You, especially when I can't always hold you tight
While kissing you goodnight. Never again we'll be
Together, so I guess this is goodbye forever.

Top Of The Class

It's amazing how you're so smart. I knew you would be
From the very start. Anyone else your age didn't
Even reach that stage. I'm so proud of whom you may become.
Because I told you "In your success you can become anyone."

It amazes me to see how quietly you learn and how
Much you know. I love to watch your brain grown.
Receiving your report cards and our awards,
Makes me proud. I would shout it to a crowd.

It's very cool that you love school because
Mommy don't wanna raise a fool.

Too Much

You have a child, you are the mother there is
No other, your child makes you look like a fool,
That isn't cool.

How are you gonna allow your child to rule over you?
You are the parent, you should know what to do.

There's no way your child should be acting like that.
Your child shouldn't make up your mind and make
Your mind go off track. Your child controls you,
And that's a fact.

Irresponsible

What kind of parent are you? Sitting around doing
Nothing while your toddler does whatever
He wants to do.

He throws things especially tantrums. He breaks
And destroys everything he sees and you just sit there.

If you don't want him, you shouldn't have
Given birth. You need to tame him because
He's out of control.

Fate Or Love

We never been nor met before yet we have
Everything in common until now that I have gotten
To know you, we like the same things and enjoy
The same activities I like to do.

Could this be that you are the one whom was
Made for me? How could this be? It seems like
We're a different root but from the same tree.

So we go out on a date, but don't stay out too late.
Just enough to get to know each other better
And see if we were meant to be together.

Beggars

Why do they always ask money from the poor?
They don't seem to be bothering the Rich.
We can barely save money to feed ourselves.
How are we supposed to feed and support other?
When we can't do for ourselves?

We're the ones whom need the help. When we
Do try to help, we gets nothing in return, but
People asking for more money and that's
Not so funny.

Most people are just greedy, begging from
The needy. Some of them are already Rich.
Ain't that bout a bitch.

Why Want More?

Who's to say, I owe you more? I give you enough
Already and I barely have anything left for
Myself. Every time I get a little income, here
You go with your hands out wanting some.

How can you be so selfish and not even care I
Have a toddler to take care of, still you refuse
To show us love.

You're taking my money and it's not even funny. Why
Are you worrying about the things I buy? @ least
I do try. My money is all you worry about. When
Things don't go your way, you scream and shout. We
Go through this every day and still I have to pay.

A Sunny Day

Today was a beautiful day, not a cloud in the sky,
Nor strong wind in the air, but a nice cool breeze
To make you feel @ ease.

It's a day to go out, play, and go have fun in the park
Until it gets dark. A nice day for a nice long walk or
Go out with friends and talk.

It's a Perfect day to go out on a date, enjoying yourself,
But not too late.

A sunny day, good for riding a bike, washing cares,
And flying a kite.

I'm Free

I'm Free! I'm Finally Free!
Now I can go home and be
With my family.

I can't believe I've been gone for so many years.
I'm so happy, I can't stop crying so many tears.

I'm free! I'm finally free!
Now I can be the person I was meant to be
And I can live for me.

Unexpected Pregnancy

A young woman, whom always went to school. She
Did all of her work, gotten good grades, never once]
Did she complain? She always participated in
Different extracurricular activities, even drama, never
Did she knew she was becoming a momma.

The option for an abortion is way past due, she felt
Bad because she didn't know what to do. Only
Adoption was her only option.

So when the day cam for her to give birth to
The baby, she knew it wasn't a maybe, since she
Didn't have anyone else because she couldn't
Raise it all by herself.

I Need A Job!

I need a Job! I need one now!
Nobody would hire me, because they think I'm too
Lazy.

I need a job! I'd go apply, but I wouldn't get
Hired, so why even try.

I need some money, but with no diploma nor experience,
What kind of job can a get? It won't be nothing I like to
Do, so forget it, until that time come than I'll have
Everything I need and my plants start growing from
A tiny little seed.

Marriage

A sacred bond between two people whom love
Each other no matter the struggle, but there
For one another.

When in a fight, agree to disagree and respect each
Other's decisions that will make it right.

Marriage is also a give and take, talk to each other
Before it's too late.

"Crazy People"

Why call them "crazy?", because they're not like you
And me? They aren't "crazy", their lives didn't turn
Out how it was meant to be.

Some People goes to school.
Some People goes to work.
Some People do both for all that it's worth.
But often times other aren't given the same opportunity.

Don't judge nor criticize, be rude, nor be cruel.
You don't know what their situation is all about,
So don't count them out.

Enzo And Chyna

Sister and brother weren't like each other.
They loved to play every day, but different
In their own way.

Enzo; he was gray and white. He was more of a kitten
Of the night because he like to sleep all day. We
Didn't bond much because he always stayed away,
He was so defensive, he liked to fight and bite.

Chyna; she was black and white. She played all day and night. She
Was a sweet kitten. She didn't like to fight.

They were very cool and made us smile. Especially
When they say in front of the tv while we watched
"Tom and Jerry". Their reactions were so cute, they
Looked like they were trying to catch "Jerry" too
And they looked confused when "Tom"
Was getting abused.

Holding Me Back

Why do you hold me back? I'm trying to get my
Life together and you keep knocking it off track.

I want to be successful too. How can you be so
Selfish and think of only you?

I want to do things and go many places, but I
Can't do that if you keep pushing me back
So many spaces.

It's Fine

There's no need to stress over things that really
Don't matter. It's a small issue so why make it
Into a big deal.

Some Problems are bigger than others, but this
Isn't one of them? So please calm down, ease you pain,
And stop straining your brain.

Most People get very sick form stress,
With you doing the same is a big mess,
And making things worse.

P.I.T.A

Children these days don't wanna listen now do
As they're told. By themselves they don't know
Which was to go and when you steer them
Right they'd always turn left.

You tell them their way isn't the best way to go.
They'll hear you talking, but then say "so",
Than realize there's no other place to go. They
Don't wanna admit they're wrong, so they
Keep on walking.

Now they feel alone and wanna come back home.
So you open the door and left them in,
Still they disrespect you, than run away again.

Deadbeat Moms

Why waste time being a deadbeat mom? If you
Give up and feel that all hope if gone, don't
Abuse them and treat them like shit
Because you can't deal with it.

Situations like this happens every day.
Moms neglect their responsibilities just to get away.

In The Mirror

Every time I look in the mirror, what do I see?
I see a beautiful person looking back @ me.

Sometimes I don't feel beautiful @ all,
Because deep down inside I feel very small.

Sometimes I can look in the mirror, tell myself
"I'm very pretty", if that's so,
How come I'm always feeling down?

There were many times before when I
Couldn't look in the mirror @ all.

Now I can't stay out of the mirror because
I love whom I see, my reflection
Looking back @ me.

The Love I Lost

The Love I Lost can never be Replaced, I can't
Believe it's true, now you're gone out of my life
For good. I don't know how I'm gonna make it
Through living my life without you.

We've been together for many years. Now that our
Family is torn apart, it hurts deep inside my heart.

I'm sorry that we have to be so far away. I'm gonna
Miss seeing your face every day. Writing letters and
Talking on the phone, only makes me wish that
You come back home.

Seizures

DAMN! Seizures have a great impact on someone's
Life. It also affect others as well. Having seizures
Are not so swell.

I have them very often and it's scary, each time I
Have one, I can lose my life.

There have been times, I've had more than one
In a day. Having seizures really gets in my way.

Medication don't keep them from coming back,
Nor is it a cure. Dealing with this really keep my
Mind off track. I wish there were a cure
Because I can't take no more.

Have You Ever?

Have you ever been part of a family, yet still feel alone?
Because family turned their backs on you because
You've grown?

Have you ever lived in a place, only to feel that you don't
Belong? And whenever you do right, people
Always say "you're wrong"?

Have you ever loved someone special, never was loved
Back and felt nothing but neglected and disrespected?
I have, I felt it all and it hurts. It led me into a lot
Of stress and depression. I even took medication
But nothing worked, so I just cried tears for many
Many years.

What's Wrong?

Why don't you talk to me? There's no reason why,
You should be so shy. It hurts me to see you
Just sit around and cry.

Please tell me, why do you cry so many tears?
Why do you have all of these fears and
Constant nightmares?

Around others; you act as if nothing's wrong, but I
Can see past all of the phony smiles that
You're not feeling so strong.

You can talk to me anytime and any day.
I just wanna help make your tears go away.

Perfect Strangers

We know of each other, but don't know each other.
We made a human being from a harmless fling.

He's a good dad, I'm a good mom.
Things will get better in time.

We struggle now, but pretty soon,
Our lives will be turned around.

Two Perfect Strangers loving the same child
And we're very proud.

Love Letter

I Love You, More than anything in this world,
Sometimes I don't act like it, but I really do wanna
Be your girl.

I imagine us being together every day and every night,
But in reality, I was holding my pillow tight.

I love you and I want you to love me, emotionally,
Unconditionally and sexually.

I was made for you and you was made for me. We should
Be together and live happily forever.

Rich with No$$$

I don't have any money, no house, no job, and no cars
But I'm living Rich just like the stars.

I don't need money to live like I'm Rich. I have
Friends and family. When we get together us
Show lots of love.

I still feel it coming from my family living with
Jesus in the heavens above and that love
Will last forever.

You Must Obey

You must obey, if you don't there is a price to pay.
If you choose not to obey, you'll be somewhere,
Where you don't belong and you'd be there
Every day without a chance to play and
Singing the same old song.

Lots of people choose to go down that road.
Some don't even care, until they would be gone
For more than a year. Than they wish they
Would've done what they were told.

Moving On

OMG! The things we've said couldn't be
Unread, well it's too late now cause I no longer
Want him to come around. In fact, I have my eyes
On someone else.

He looks better and more independent.
He's so kind and so sweet, He's a really good friend.
One day I hope we can become something more.
He caught my eyes when he walked through the door.
I almost dropped my phone on the floor.

I Got It Bad

There's no need to be in denial. I love your style,
Hearing your name, and seeing your picture makes
My mind and body run wild and makes me smile.

When I'm not near you, I fantasize about you all
Night, than I start to toy around with myself
Because I refuse to give my body to someone else.

I'm always thinking about you every minute of
The day, wondering if you're ok. While watching
TV, I only see myself looking back @ me.

Irreplaceable

I Love my children, more than anyone nor
Anything in this world.

Without them, I don't know where I'll be.
I'm just glad to have them with me.

They are the sunshine in my day
And the moonlight and stars @ night.

These are my babies, even when they get old.
We keep each other warm whenever it gets cold.

I can't see myself living without them, and them
Without me. Each and every one of them
Will always be my baby.

God's Miracle

A young child whom has been sick and in the
Hospital for months feeling so weak, she don't
Have enough energy to speak.

Not only that she can't talk, but she also can't walk.
As she lies in a coma, her family stands by
Her and pray.

One day to her mother's surprise, she slowly
Opened up her eyes, than after a week,
She started to speak.

After a while when she was talking, she
Started walking. Her mom and dad was
Having the best feeling they ever had.

Thieving Angels

Whom would've thought that nice and obedient?
Children (or so we thought) lies, steals, cheats
And bully other kids.

What happened to the children we've grown to know
And love, whom God has sent us from the heavens above?

Almost every day we heard different things
About how, what, where and who they stole from.
Some kids today are just dumb.

Favoritism

Two children belong to the same mother,
But one is being loved more so than the other.

One child gets all of the attention and never misused,
While the other is being ignored and abused.

It's not fair, that their mother don't even care, that she
Loves one more than the other, or maybe she isn't
Aware that her love isn't equally shared.

Two children whom belong to the same father.
It's a shame, all he do is scream and holler.

He takes one child out, but the other, he don't even
Bother. He gives one a quarter, and the other,
He gives a whole dollar.

One of the two, gets treated like a queen,
While the other rarely be seen, and don't
Know what to do.

I'm Me

Quit trying to change me. No matter what you say
Or do, no matter what we go through, as long as
I live, I'm me.

I can be nice and I can be mean. I'm like two
People in one body. Take your pick; which one
Do you wanna see? Because I have more than
One personality.

It doesn't matter what you say nor think, I'm
Forever gonna be me. Many people tell me
"You're crazy, you have issues, and you need therapy."

No medicine, nor therapy will change who
I am for I have tried, it just took away some
Of my pride, but not the people I have inside,
I'm forever gonna be me.

Depression Hurts

Depression is like a roller coaster ride.
Your emotions goes up and down, and your head
Spins round and round, you'll never know
What you'll feel inside.

Depression; it can either make or break you,
Sometimes you don't know what to do.
It can also make you feel like you're alone,
As if all of your hopes and dreams are gone.

Depression can also cause you to isolate and rarely
Decides to participate. Most people say
"That only medication can take the depression away."

This isn't true, medication can only make it adjusted.
Most medications can't be trusted. May people
Deal with depression every day.

Not only depression effect you; it can have a great impact
On your family and friends too.

The Reverend's Daughter

A young woman whom wanted to explore the world.
It wasn't as exciting as she wanted it to be. She
Was mistreated, used, and most definitely abused.

In the beginning; she thought everything was great.
She shopped and traveled from state to state.

When things went wrong, she wanted to go back home,
But she thought it was too late.

When the chance for her to go back home came,
She packed her things and got on the next plane.

She thought her life as a Reverend's daughter
Was expected to be so perfect, but when she
Got back home, she realized leaving
Wasn't worth it.

We're Gonna Make It

We may be struggling now, but in a little while,
Our lives will be turned around.

If we try to do it apart, neither of us would know
Where to start.

As long as we work together, things will work
Out for the better.

We don't have enough money to give, but soon,
We'll have a place to live.

During the while, as we struggle, all we can do now
Is pray that everything will be ok.

I need you, just as much as you need me. We have to
Stay strong for our family tree.

Every day I cry tears, hoping our troubles
Won't last for years.

Our kids need us, we have to work together so
We can make it, not break it, and that's a must.

Rejected

I feel so alone, I have nobody to call my own.
I tried to be real and tell him how I feel. Only to
Find out he whom is special to me, wasn't the person
I'd thought he'd be.

Now I feel bad to know he doesn't care, while
Lying there on his chest, he wasn't even aware,
I was crying my every tear.

Even though the sex is great, it can't continue
Because it's a big mistake. At first, I thought it
Was all about fun. Nine months later, I
Gave birth to a healthy handsome son.

Now that I know, I refuse to let my feelings show.
I shouldn't have allowed our meaningless sex
To even start because he won't let me into his heart.

Until It's Gone

"You'll never know what you've got until it's gone."
You're going away, but you're not gonna stay.
It's only for a little while, then you're coming back,
Try telling my heart that. When I think about you
Leaving, I just sit back and cry.

If only you knew how I really do feel about you, and
Know they are very real and true. Throughout all of
The times, I have pushed you away. I really
Wanted you to stay.

I understand you have to go because of work,
But deep inside, it still hurt. You didn't even leave yet,
But I'm already missing you and want you
To come back.

Your warm hugs and tender kiss, I'd most
Definitely miss. I would be missing you every
Minute of the day that you're gone, but the
Real questions is...will you miss me too?
While I'm sitting @ home alone.

Back & Forth

For many years, I've been back & forth crying tears.

My back & forth depression is really having a great
Impact on my life.

I'm starting to forget some things that are very important.

I feel very bad when I make people upset
Because I forget.

Sometimes my mind wanders off track, but
Eventually it'll come back.

There are quite a few times I lay down and cry
Without knowing the reason why, because I have a
Lot of things on my mind running around all
@ The same time.

Not only has my medication made me drowsy,
But being depressed makes me tired too.
It hurts so bad, I don't know what to do.

Phat Bitches

I am one of the many "Phat Bitches" in our city.
But why are the skinny bitches worried so much
About me? I am happy. No matter what they say,
I am me every day and I'm "Grown and sexy."

Why should I feel shame, because the skinny
Bitches called me out of my name? I look and
Feel good, just as I should.

If they have to try to put me down to build up their
Self-esteem, than they aren't as confident as
They may seem.

I've been "phat" my whole life.
Never once have I been "skinny",
I'm proud to be "phat", and I don't care
Who has a problem with that.

Tell Me Why

I have a lot of pain hidden inside
That I refuse to let outside
Because I do have too much pride.
Sometimes I feel good, as I should,
Other times I'm depressed,
Maybe even stressed.

My life is so complicated, it's hard to explain,
Because I have too much stuff on my brain.
Then I start crying for hours sometimes
Even days. My emotions change in so many ways.

When I start to feel bad around others. I don't
Want them to know, so I don't allow
My tears to show.

Someone...Tell me why aren't I entitled to be in
A relationship because of all of the things
I'm going through, I think this is the perfect
Time for me to be with someone, so they can
Help me get my mind off of all my troubles.

Tell me why can't I have the family that I always
Dream of having, because I'm not the person
Other people want me to be? Alone or not alone
Sadly, I'm always gonna be me.

Getting Played

A young girl whom loves deeply, loves a man
And hopes he feels the same way, or @
Least even care. She stayed awake for him,
Even when she was sleepy.

Later she realized he really didn't care
And her hopes, dreams and fantasies
Wasn't going anywhere.

She wanted to cry, but she had so much pain
In her heart that not one tear drop
Fell from her eye.

You Don't Know Me

You don't know me, you act like you do,
But you really don't. I know you want to,
But you won't.

So you can do whatever you wanna do,
Say whatever you wanna say, but you ain't hurting me.
I'm gonna live to see another day.

Another day for me to put you in your place,
So you can stay out of my face,
Because if you don't, then I'm just
Gonna catch a case.

A Hero

A hero is more than just someone whom
Saves lives and fight for our country.

A hero can also be someone
Whom comes into a person's or people lives
To mend their broken hearts.

A hero can also be considered as a
Person that's admired. Here on earth,
For all that its worth, my hero is my son.

I wish

I wish I didn't love him, because he
Doesn't love me. I try to get him to feel the same
Way about me as I do, but I have to face the
Facts that it's true. I'll never hear the words
"I love you, when I'm sad and feeling down
My mood changes whenever he comes around.

I've tried other relationships hoping to move on and
Put him behind, but how can I do that when he's
Always in my heart and on my mind.

I wish he would open his heart and let me in,
I want to be more than just his friend,
Because the love I have for him will never end.

Emotional Roller Coaster

I love him, I can no longer deny it,
I can't get over him. I know
Because I Tried it.

I tried other relationships, but when we're apart,
He's always on my mind and forever in my heart.
He's been there from the start.

I tried to hate him, as if I didn't care,
But my feelings for him isn't going anywhere.
Although I tried to walk away. I think about him
And cry every day.

Make It Last

Can we start over? A new beginning.
A new life for the both of us.
Why can't we make it last?
Put all of the arguing in the past.

We have to put up with each other forever,
sp why not be together. We're not strangers.
We do have a family.

A child to love and protect? Don't forget,
That without us he wouldn't be here,
If we can share him, why can't we share our love?
In a new life and this time we'll make it last.

Rainy Days

It rains every day, nobody knows why,
There's dark, heavy clouds in the sky.

Rainy days always gets in the way.
Where is the sunshine, so we can go out to play?

I wish the rain stop.
I can't wait until the last drop.

The water is rising so high and deep
Nobody can get some peaceful sleep.

Rain leaks into houses and bars.
Outside so flooded, people
Can't get to their cars.
Students going to school
Can't get very far.

Now that the rain is gone
And the sun has shone
The ground is dry
With white clouds
With a clear blue sky.

I'm Missing You

It's been a long time
Since I remember
When you were mine.

Not being able to see you
Nor talk to you every day
Makes me wish you never went away.

Being in your arms every night
Made me feel just right
Especially when you held me tight.

Looking into your eyes
Is like watching the sunrise.
I often cry because I miss you.
I hope you miss me too.

Some people says that I should
"Move on & let go", but they
Don't know how I feel.
My love for you is for real.

Come back to me, so we could
Have our own family, the way
We should be.

Every day I'm reminiscing
And imagining I hear your voice
Since I don't see you anymore
So, I don't have a choice

I'm Ready

I haven't been so sure about nothing before.
Every day I see pregnant women and new moms
With their baby. I wish one of them were me,
But I was denied the chance to extend my family.

I still have the baby furniture from my first baby.
I still have the crib, blankets, and the play pin.
I can't wait until I can use it again.

It doesn't matter if they baby is a boy
Because he would bring me so much joy
And if the baby is a girl
She would forever change my world.

I miss the feeling of looking @ my baby
Inside of me and watching my stomach
Get as big as it could be.

I don't care what anyone else says
Or thinks about me, all I know
Is that I'm ready.

Hard Times

We struggle in so many ways.
We've some good and many bad days,
But just to let you know,
I'll be here, always.

Don't feel bad if you can't play your part.
If we keep trying, we can make a new start.

I don't want you to feel alone.
We're not gonna struggle forever
Because we're in this together.

Being Fooled

He cheated on me. He acted like he didn't care,
But little did he know that, I was aware,
Because when I walked into the bedroom,
I found used condoms and another
Woman's underwear there.

I can't believe, she would cheat, while me
Working hard, sweating from the heat.
Making sure we have food to eat.
I had to work an extra hour, but
When I got home, she wasn't alone.
I found her and another
Man in my shower.

So they both cheated, it's not complicated so
If they can't commit to each other, they
Should part ways and look forward to
Better days.

My Sick Baby

One day, I got a phone call from my son's
School saying "I have to pick him up because
He's complaining his stomach hurt." when I
Brought him home, it only gotten worse.

I rushed him to the emergency
And I stayed there with him all night.
Before I left, I gave him a kiss
And tucked him in tight.

My Sick Baby, depending on a nurse
Instead of me and I'm depending on God
To stay by our side.

They very next day, I went to visit him.
When I got there, I was so happy to see him play.
Thank you Jesus for watching my baby.

I was very happy when the nurse
Said these six words...
"He can go home with me."

Go Away

Please Go Away. I don't
Want to see you another day.

You have hurt me many times before.
My heart gotten cold and I don't
Love you anymore.

I get so annoyed when I see
Your name on the "caller ID"
Because I don't want you calling me.
We have a child, but we aren't family.

How dare you come by, and unexpected,
After you made us feel neglected!
Don't be surprised when you get rejected.

Lock It Down

A young woman looking for love in all the wrong
Places and seen many faces. She been up, down,
And all around town, she had so many friends, she
Don't know where the line ends.

Although, she went searching from love, all she found was lust.
She had to turn away from that life and that was a must.
So, her search for a special friend was put to an end.

She decided to put that part of her life in the past.
She didn't search for love anymore. She stayed to
Herself until love found her and make it last.

The Man Whom Cried

He fell off the bed, and hit his head.
Why don't you cry? Asked his daughter
Because I'm a man, he answered.

He fell out of the chair without losing a single hair.
Why don't you cry? Asked his daughter
Because I'm a man, he answered.
He got hit with a brick when he picked
Up a stick and lightening flashed
When he crashed. Why don't you cry?
Asked his daughter, because I'm a man,
He answered.

He watched his beautiful daughter
Become a beautiful bride. He became
Excited and emotional inside.
And that's the day the man cried.

I'm Coming

You said, "You wanted a good man."
Now that you have him you
Treat him like shit.
Well I'm putting your
Selfishness and ungratefulness
To an end, because I'm coming.

All he do for you,
And the shit you
Put him through,
Though, he still care
And willing to take you anywhere.

He just wants your
Honesty and loyalty, still you're unhappy
And you act as if
He isn't worthy.

A man who loves you and your children
That didn't come from his seed,
Deserves all of your love indeed,
But since you don't understand
I'm coming, to take your man.

A New Year

A new year is now here
Time to start off Brand new
So everything in the past
We should leave it there.

Things I didn't do, I'm
Gonna try and put an effort to,
And try to get done because
It won't get accomplished by anyone.

I have future plans for my life
I won't accomplish those goals
Just sitting around everywhere without a care,
And let me life pass me by, then I'll really
Be sitting around wondering why.

A new year means,
I have to finish what I've started
So, I won't end up brokenhearted.

Ain't Getting it Right?

I don't mean to be rude,
But you have a crazy ass attitude.
I don't understand, why don't
You take it out on your man.

It's not my fault, he needs to be taught
Because he keeps performing
The same way every day and night.
You need to tell him that he
Ain't giving it right.

Every day you got something "smart" to say.
Why don't you just get a book and take a look,
In the classified, it'll teach you
Other ways to get satisfied.

I'm so tired of your attitude
Every day and night,
Tell your man, you ain't getting it right.

WWJD?

Where's the faith?
Life is tough, trying to
Make it is rough.

Moving around from
Place to place, feeling
Bad and don't want nobody
In your face.

Telling you what to do,
How to be, how to dress,
Your priorities is
In such a mess.

Can't work because of struggles,
Very little money with
No place to go.

Bills stacked so high
They almost reach the sky.
Don't have enough food stamps
To buy something to eat.
Looks like we're gonna get
Put out on the street.

Nobody understands
The hurt and pain
You go through.
Just ask this one question...
What Would Jesus Do?

My Husband

A man whom loves me unconditionally
And not care what anyone has to say,
Just keeps me smiling all day.

A man whom is kind, gentle
Keeps his hands to himself,
And don't fall in love with anyone else.

A man whom accepts and love my kids
As his own, just as much as he loves me
So we'll be a family.

A man whom is honest, always tells the truth.
And never insecure about
The friends I have next door.

A man whom stays out of trouble,
Whenever needed he's there on the double
If things on his mind, he's willing
To sit down and talk, other
Than arguing and getting up to walk.

A man whom is willing to help
Me as much as he can
Is what is expected from my husband?

Chauvinism

Why do men act that way?
Many people have sex every day.
Having sex requires
A male and a female
So what difference does it make
After it happens it's already too late.

It seems as though, if a
Boy have sex it's alright,
But if a girl have sex
Everyone wants to fight.

When men have sex
With multiple women, it's all good,
But when a woman have sex
With multiple men, she's
A whore of the hood
We need to be treated
Equal just as we should.

Women become Doctors
They can get recognition
But let a male become a nurse
He'll get laughed @ and treated the worse.
Patients still gets the same attention
And not be misused, so
Why does it matter?
Which career they choose.

Grateful

You are not our fathers,
But yet, you still choose
To be there when nobody else care

Sometimes we argue
But still I love you
Although I don't show it,
But I do and I'm
Thankful we have you.

When we're hungry
You make sure we get food.
Even if it's just a piece of meat,
You still make sure that we eat.

You are so helpful and kind
Anyone would be glad
To have you in their life.
I'm very grateful
That you're in mine
Thank you.

Slow Down

You're moving a little too fast
Get time to know each other
Or the relationship won't last.

Since you're so impatient
And can't wait,
Go find someone
Whom wants it
As bad as you.
I'm not supposed
To do it because
You want to.

You are a good
Person that I would admit
I introduce you to
Some of my family
Until I know more
About you, that's it

We haven't yet
Went out nor
Spent quality time together
You keep on rushing
And trying to pressure
Me than you ain't
Getting Sugar, honey, Iced Tea.

Quit Now

It stinks, it's disgusting
And it's nasty especially
When you kissing me.
It feels like I'm kissing
An ashtray, who
Would want to kiss that every day.
I'm not supposed to be around smoke anyway.

The smell on your breath clogs my nose
Whenever you come near me
The stench gets on my clothes.
I enjoy your company whenever you're near
But not when that smell is everywhere.
If you can't accept that than stay over there.

I really care about you,
But I also care about
My lungs too. This is my
Life and I want it to last
And I don't want this to be
The reason for me noticing it
You may not love yours,
But I love my life
And I am blessed
I refuse to lose it over some mess.

Always Be First

All Christians know that Jesus is first
Before any human being
Especially a man for all
That it's worth, you will
Always be first

You are my best friend
Until the very end.
You have been for many years
I can always talk to you even
When my eyes are filled with tears.

Your children are so great
I love them as my nieces
And my nephew, because
You're more than a friend
I love you as my sister too.
We'll always be together
No matter what we go through.
Our friendship is forever
And that's true

Most friends I had
Since I was a child,
We've grown apart
No visit nor phone call
Just "Hi & bye" that's all
And never looked back,
But we moved from
Place to place
And never lost contact.

Follow Your Heart

When a talent is found,
Keep it and use it,
It may turn your life around

What's boring to others?
Can be enjoyable to you
Don't stop because
People don't like what you do

Other people opinions
Shouldn't matter at all,
Especially to those whom
Won't catch you when you fall

If you have the opportunity to
Do something, you shouldn't
Just let it fly by.

Why should you care what people believe
They don't care what you can achieve
Do what you feel is right for you
Don't let anyone tell you what you can't do.

Unhappy

Unsatisfied in a relationship
That I don't want. I don't
Wanna hurt his feelings
I'd just put on a front.

I like him a lot
I know he likes me
But he's not the
Kind of man he should be
I have better satisfaction
Eating chocolate candy.

There's no passion
Not intimacy
How could I say
"I don't want him
To be with me."
Without being rude
Because I have
An attitude?

He appears to be
Nice and kind,
But I no longer
Want him to be mine.
It's a waste of a phone call
And it's a waste of my time.

Too Much

Although I throw things
In the trash everyday
Still I have a lot of shit
That's in my way.

My space so crowded
When I try to walk
I always trip over
Something

If not clothes, than shoes
Or bags. What I'll throw
Away next I can't choose.

Everything I have I need
I can't keep throwing
Everything away,
Then I won't have
Nothing @ all but
I don't have a lot
Of space so things
Are going to be all
Over the place.

Just Me

Why can't I just be me?
For the sake of being me
It's like everything I do
Is wrong to you.

There's a problem
With my looks.
The way I wear
My hair, why
Should you care?
I have nobody
To impress, I love
The way I dress.

I shouldn't have to
Change me
Because I'm not
Whom you want me to be.

"Mommy And Me Day"

When I have extra
Money to spare
I pick a day
For my son and I
To go anywhere
It's just a day for
Us to share.

Sometimes we go to
Basketball games,
Concerts, movies,
And sometimes
We'll just go out
To eat @ a restaurant

I love to spend
My spare time
With my son

I've heard people
Say that parents
Shouldn't be friends
Or hang out with
Their children

When I hang
Out with my son
We have fun!
I love each minute
Of the day we spend together
Because our love last forever.

Got Screwed?

I'm not talking about tools.
I'm talking about how people
Promise shit and you expect it
That they wanna back down
And switch their words around.

If you made a promise
Stick to your word
Others know what they heard.

People making plans
To choose what they
Want to do. Thinking
Everything going to
Go your way

Now you're feeling
Bad and ashamed
Because people wanna
Think your life
Is one big game
But they're the
Blame.

I bet now you feel
Hopeless and confused
Because you got screwed.

Family Secrets

Why didn't you tell me?
That I wasn't really
Part of your family.
When I was a

Child running wild
I was so happy
As I could be
Now I feel empty.

Who am I?
Where do I come from?
Why didn't you tell
Me from the very start?
Now that I have grown
To love you, I don't know
What to do, you have broken my heart.

How can I tell my children
That those they love is
Nothing more than just a friend?
All of this time I was raised by strangers
Yet you told me to stay away from them,
What do I do, now that I found out
That you're one of them too?
Who is my real dad and mom?
Don't tell me it's a long story
Because we have a lot of time.

Unappreciated

Everything I do is never
Good enough for you.
I cook, I clean
And all you do
Is just be mean.

Sometimes I buy things
With my own money
And yet you treat me
As if I was a dummy
And I don't find that funny.

Every time I do right
You say I'm wrong
Because I don't
Do it your way.
You act this way every day.

All of the time.
You treat me as a maid,
All that I do for you
I should be getting paid,

I just want you to appreciate
Me just as I am
Not for what you
Want me to be
Then we'll be able to communicate.

Feed Me Now

When I'm hungry
With a big appetite
I don't want a sample
With a little flavor.
I need a meal which
I can savor.
Fill me up right.

I like my meat
Strong, thick, tender,
And so juicy that
My hands get wet.
I want a meal
I'll never forget.

I don't get hungry every day.
When I have an appetite, I can eat.
All day and all night
Sometimes I get hungry
When I'm trying to sleep.

I can't get any rest
Because of my appetite.
I won't be satisfied
Until it's done right.
When I get hungry,
Don't make me wait
Otherwise I won't feel so great

Love Me or Leave Me

How dare you treat me this way?
You yell, control, and beat me every day.
I am your wife, this is not how
I pictured my life.

How can you be amused @
The way I'm being abused?
By the way you act,
You can kill me, and that's a fact,
You call me "Lazy", but you won't
Even help me with our baby.
It's sad that I can't dress
Myself like a lady.
No make-up, dress, nor blouse,
Just pants and shirts I can't even wear skirts.

I want to be loved unconditionally and be happy
You won't allow me to get my hair done, go out
With my family and friends because you say
"You're my only one." When will the abuse ends? How can
You allow your children to watch you abuse their mom?
I'm fed up going through this all of the time.

I love you and I want you to love me too,
But if you can't and won't stop abusing me
Sign the divorce papers and leave me be.

Can't Take No More

We've been married for years.
We were happy, but now
I just sit around crying many tears.

I awake from a good night's sleep
Prepared your food, but you
Don't wanna eat.
I felt it was very rude

You always leave me
At home alone,
But when you are home
You'd always be on the phone

On our anniversary
Instead of spending it with me,
You'd rather go with friends
And party.

What happened to our family?
It's like you don't wanna
Be with me anymore.
So I'll pack my things
And go out the door
Because in this marriage
I can't take no more.